TO THE MILL AND BACK

a novel by

Bill Savage

To the Mill and Back

ISBN 979-8-35090-194-8 (Print)
ISBN 979-8-35090-195-5 (eBook)

BOOK
ONE

1: BIRTH OF A BOBBIN BOY

The glass bottles rattled in their wooden shells as the soda delivery truck chugged up the hill.

The truck was a lot like its driver – dirty and weather-beaten. They were carrying glass bottles of varying sizes – eight, sixteen, and thirty-two ounces – filled with carbonated concoctions with high sugar content. It was the summer of 1948, and nobody back then was interested in a zero-calorie soft drink.

A seventeen-year old boy, the sweat dripping down his back and beading on his forehead as he walked up the hill just after noon, could only fantasize about getting his taste buds around the content of those bottles. Sure, they were warm now, packed into the back of the truck, but soon they would find their way into a cooler at some little corner grocery store, where they would turn into something cold that would taste awfully good on a hot day.

"Boy, could I go for the pause that refreshes now!"

It hadn't been a good week for this young fellow. The school year had just ended, and his grades were best forgotten. He was a year away from graduating – or at least he hoped so!

But until then, he had one more summer to go, and he wasn't quite sure what he was going to do with it. When he was younger, the end of school provided him and his friends with endless hours to grab a few sticks so they could go out and hunt imaginary Germans in the nearby tall grass.

But now, at seventeen, he had more expensive interests – from a cold soft drink on up – that could only be satisfied if he got a job.

He wasn't from a wealthy family – his father worked at a small garage, while his mother usually raced through the laundry and her other domestic chores quickly enough each day to catch a few soap operas on the radio.

So if he was to ever get any closer to getting a car, or to being able to buy his own pack of smokes now and then, he had to have a job. He knew he wasn't going to get rich; he just wanted some pocket change.

But for now, he and his empty pockets were just walking, right past the little grocery with the cooler full of Cokes, Seven-ups, Pepsis, and Hires Root Beers he couldn't afford. His mouth grew drier. He felt overheated. It was pretty hot for June – probably in the mid-eighties and rising – and he was starting to feel kind of sick.

But maybe if he kept walking, he'd come across a place where he could knock on the door, go inside, get a drink of water, and then ask the woman at the front desk if they were hiring any workers for the summer. Walking and knocking. Walking and knocking some more. That was the only way to get a job – and a cool drink – in 1948. And it was the only way he could think of to solve his problem.

So he kept walking, his heavy cotton trousers sticking to his sweaty legs now, his back a watery mess, past endless ribbons of little houses; they were small, square-looking wooden houses, just like the one he lived in with his parents and a younger brother. The houses were all like that in this town. They had been company houses once, thrown together with wood and nails for next to nothing as housing for coal miners and factory workers. Now, with the war over and lots of money supposedly floating around, they sold for crazy, outlandish prices. He'd heard that somebody in his neighborhood had actually just sold one for three-thousand bucks!

He trudged up a hill, the scent of dirty, caged-up dogs wafting from every other backyard. His neck was sweaty now, matting up the edges of the hair on the back of his head. His feet were burning inside his heavy, black leather shoes.

At the top of the hill, he noticed a large building, and this one wasn't made of wood. He'd seen it before, but he'd never actually walked near the place. So when he got up close to it, he was amazed at how big it was.

Compared to the houses nearby, it was a monolith. It was dark brown, and made of some sort of stone. It rose at least five stories above the pavement, and it took up a full city block. It had row after row of small, frosted glass windows.

Smoke – or maybe it was steam – belched from at least two openings on the roof. He didn't hear any noise at first, but as he got to within perhaps thirty feet of the building, he began to hear a rumble, which turned into a more of a hum as he got closer.

He looked up to the roof and saw a sign, in large yellow letters. He'd seen it before, from a distance, when it lit up the city's night sky:

"BLAKE SILK MILL."

For many a postwar young man and woman, those thirteen letters spelled opportunity. A presence in the town since the late nineteenth century, the mill had, during World War II, churned out material for soldiers' and sailors' uniforms, for parachutes, and for anything else the war effort needed. Now it was back to its original purpose, providing textiles for a country full of people ready to buy new clothes for all those babies who had been born around the end of the war.

Yes, the big sign still called it a "silk mill," but Blake was, in fact, a robust, roaring piece of the booming American postwar economy, a humming, churning dynamo on this hill, running three shifts for five days a week, and whatever else was needed over the weekend.

The young man looked up at the sign again, shuddered a bit at its magnificence, and decided to walk another hundred or so feet until he got to what appeared to be the mill's main entrance. A gleaming brass sign there had the name of the mill engraved into it, in block letters, in almost imperial fashion. "BLAKE SILK MILL." Next to the sign was a heavy wood-and-glass door.

He looked around, wondering whether he should go in. He paused, and then, about fifty feet away, he saw black man in his mid-fifties, dressed in dark blue working clothes. All factory workers in those days wore dark blue working clothes.

At first, he didn't even consider saying anything to him. In his town, in those days, white teenagers seldom even saw a black adult on the streets; rarer still was any sort of verbal interaction. But he had no idea who he should see about applying for a job, and there wasn't anybody else around to ask.

"Excuse me," he said. "Uh ... where would I go to ... you know ... fill out a job application?"

He took a few steps toward the man, who was carrying a large, empty trash can, the contents of which he had just tossed into what looked like an incinerator. The man looked at him, but didn't say anything. Instead, the man crooked his index finger and motioned to him to come over.

As he approached the man, the man opened what appeared to be a service door of some type. The next thing he knew, the teenager felt as if he was standing inside of a barn in Oklahoma after somebody had opened the door during a tornado.

First, he heard an unmistakable *"WHOOSH!"*

And then he heard what could only be described as the very soundtrack of post-war American industrial progress ... the roar of what must have been a million rotating and twisting and grinding cams and gears and rotors, pounding out a symphony of auditory revolutions that made the boy wonder if every gosh-darned factory on the East Coast had somehow had its sound piped into the hallways of this five-story roar-a-torium!

Silk mill? Those words had always sounded so tranquil, so serene. They evoked images of dainty Asian women working by hand to weave together shiny pieces of shimmering textile.

This place sounded as if they were blasting out half the freakin' Appalachian mountains in there!

The black man put the trash can inside, then closed the door. The man wiped his own brow, from which poured more sweat than the youngster had seen in his life.

"Woo-wee!" the man said. "Man, it's getting' hot! Now, what was that you said, young fella? Somethin' about a job?"

"Uh … I was just … I was just wondering if they're taking applications back there," he said, pointing to the main entrance.

"How old are you?" the man said.

"Seventeen."

"Oh, well, you ain't got a chance at workin' on them machines in there," he said. "Gotta be eighteen for that. Besides, some a them folks in there … they're gonna hafta carry them outta here, ya know? They's lifers! They ain't never gonna give up the jobs they got in there."

The boy, still a bit overwhelmed by the noise he'd heard, shrugged his shoulders, nodded, and started to walk away.

"Yeah, sure," he said in dejection. "I understand. Thanks anyway."

"Now jes' wait a minute!" the man shouted back at him. "I don't recall tellin' you to walk away from here with your chin down around your belt buckle, did I? And just when did I say they ain't *takin'* applications?"

He turned back around. "Uh … I thought you said …"

"Well you didn't let me *finish*!" the man said. "I said they ain't gonna hire you to work on them machines in there. But they *do* got other jobs in there. For one thing, they do hire some young guys to paint the place over the summer. And they got some more grass in the back, so they bring in some young fellas to pull weeds and that sort of thing. Maybe you could go in and ask about that!"

He wasn't impressed. Cut grass? Pull weeds? He could do that at home.

The man glared at him.

"Ain't for you, eh?" the man growled. "Ain't the paintin' and pullin' type, eh? Well then, let's see … you oughta be … that's right … you could go in and see if they need any bobbin boys."

He moved his head back. *Bobbin boys?* What the heck did *that* mean? It sounded kind of girly. What did a bobbin boy *do* … put pins in women's hair?

"You know what a bobbin boy does?" the man said.

He shook his head.

"It ain't that bad a job," the man said. "See, what happens is, they get this yarn from … well, I don't know where they get it … from over in India or someplace, and then they run it through these machines. Don't ask me what the heck happens when they run it through there. Seems like a lot of commotion and noise and electrical power when all they really is doin' is running things through a machine … and to me, it looks the same when it comes back out! But anyway … once the yarn goes through the machine, they need somebody to take the empty spools … they call `em bobbins; don't ask me why … and clean `em up so they can send `em back to wherever they got `em."

"Sounds like an easy job."

"I don't know, I ain't never done it," the man said. "I know they got some folks doin' it who ain't too bright, if you know what I mean. You know … fellas who can't work nowhere else. But sometimes they got some kids like you … fellas who ain't legal age to work on the machines … sometimes they got kids like you doin' it. And it ain't bad work if you's savin' up for whatever."

"And I can fill out an application in there?" he said, pointing to the office.

"Yes sir!" the man said. "Now I ain't guaranteein' they's lookin' for bobbin boys at the present time. They might send you home with your tail between your legs. But it's worth a shot, man!"

"Well ... yeah," the boy said. "Thank you." He thought maybe he should add a "sir" on the end, but he hadn't ever had this long a conversation with a black man before. He didn't know the protocol.

"So get in there and get to it," the man said. "You already showed you got the will to work ... now go in there and get yourself some walkin-around money!"

And then the man opened the door again, and the wheels of industry roared again, dwarfing any other sound being made on the street. As he headed inside, he wondered how long a fellow could work in there without going deaf. But the janitor – at least he *assumed* the man was the janitor – he seemed to hear okay.

He took a deep breath. He wasn't very good at just walking into offices and asking for applications. He always thought they were going to laugh at him. But something inside him told him to give it a try.

"What the heck?" he thought. "At least they probably have a water fountain in there!"

• • •

He opened the heavy door and took a few steps into a narrow hallway reception area. Thick glass separated that area from the office workers on the other side, and there were no signs posted telling visitors what to do. So he just stood there for a moment until a woman in her thirties noticed him, pushed open a sliding window, and smiled.

"Hello, there," she said. "May I help you?"

He noticed that there was a water cooler – the really fancy type, with the heavy, big glass tank and the little cone-shaped paper cups – in the office area behind the woman. More than a job application, he wanted a drink from that water cooler, but he knew they didn't just let kids come in and refresh themselves without good reason.

"Uh ... yes ... uh ... I was wondering ... are you ..."

His mouth got as dry as he could ever remember it being.

"... are you ... are you hiring? For the summer, I mean?"

"Summer work?" she said. "Let me see."

She closed the sliding window and approached two men behind her. They appeared to be arguing between themselves. One of the men was in his fifties, short, bald, a little paunchy, and was wearing a short-sleeved white shirt with a tie and dark pants. The other man was taller, also in his fifties, but he was wearing a light blue shirt and no tie. The argument began right about the time the woman opened the window to greet him, and it was still going on. But he couldn't hear what they were arguing about.

The woman approached them, and pointed toward this potential applicant. The man in the blue shirt then pointed at him as well, and then he pointed back at the other man. The argument then resumed.

At that, another woman opened a nearby door in order to drag a box out of the office area. When she did, he was able to hear some of the argument going on behind the glass.

"More ... always more!" said the man in the tie.

"Well I can't run this department with less," said the other man.

"How many you sayin' you need?"

"At least one, maybe two. We got enough of everything else ... we just need more boys!"

The door closed. He stood there, the water cooler still in sight, like some sort of oasis. Then he noticed that the two men had stopped arguing, and that they had started looking at him. Meanwhile, the woman was now doing the talking. He couldn't hear what she said, but she kept pointing back at him. And then *all three of them* started looking back through the window at him!

He certainly was the focus of something, wasn't he? But all he could think of was getting to that water cooler!

The woman returned and opened the window. "Umm ... young man ... do you have any experience as a bobbin boy?"

Until a few minutes earlier, he had never even heard those words used together. But something told him that to get a job ... not to mention a drink! … he should mine the brief knowledge the janitor – or whoever that black fellow was – had bestowed upon him, and become one of the world's foremost experts on bobbin boys!

"You mean, cleanin' the empty spools?" he said. "I know a little about it."

The window closed again. The two men and a woman talked some more. Then the man in the tie walked away, the woman sat back down in her chair, and the man in the blue shirt emerged through the door, as the thirsty teen stood in the tiny hallway and awaited his fate.

"You lookin' for work?" the man grumbled as he popped through the door.

He nodded.

"Summer work?" the man said.

He nodded.

"Bobbin boy?"

Another nod.

Three nods got him a piece of paper and a pencil. But the piece of paper was a job application, and after seeing it, his rear end fell into the one seat they had in the hallway. He filled out the application and gave it to the woman behind the window. A few minutes later, he saw the woman give it to the man in the blue shirt, who then started heading back toward the door.

But he still hadn't gotten to that water cooler!

The man in the blue shirt came out of the door again, holding the job application in one hand.

"Okay, here's the deal," the man said gruffly. "Be here eight o'clock tomorrow morning. Stop off here to do some paperwork for the government, and then we'll take you upstairs. Any questions?"

For the first time in his life, he'd been given a job offer! A seminal moment in a young man's life, right? One he'd always remember.

"Well," he said with a gulp. "I was wondering. Could I have … a drink?"

The man's eyes widened. "A drink?" he said. "You mean, water?"

"Uh-huh."

The man shrugged. "Well, yeah … sure … go on in. That's it? No other questions. Just, 'Can I have a drink?'"

"I'm pretty thirsty," he said. "It's hot out there."

So they walked into the office, where he *finally* got to the water cooler. The triangular drinking cup barely held enough water to quench the thirst of a small bird, but it was enough to make the boy feel as if he'd emerged from the desert and come upon a cool lake. The thirst-quenching effect of the bottled water made him realize that, apparently, he had been offered, and had accepted, a job!

He wanted a second cup of water, but, hey, they just offered him a job! He didn't want to press his luck, so he didn't dare ask.

"So, you be here at eight," the man said. "If you're late, we'll probably just kick your ass out and send you home. I'll bet your old man would have a fit if he heard that!"

Did this fellow knew his father or something?

"Sure … I'll be here at eight."

He started to leave, and the man in the blue shirt began to head for another exit at the rear of the office. But then he turned and yelled back toward his newest employee.

"Hey kid," the man said. "Ain't you gonna ask what you'll be doin'?"

Based on everything he'd heard, he knew what what he'd be doing. But in a strange way, both he and the man in the blue shirt seemed to be aware that it required a formal declaration, as if bestowing the title on him would somehow place him within the realm of that designation, and make it, in this thunderous world of a silk mill, official.

"Bobbin boy!" the blue-shirted man roared. "Tomorrow at this time, you're a bobbin boy!"

• • •

His parents were only mildly impressed when he told them he was starting work the next day. He figured they'd have a lot of questions, but they mainly seemed to want to know when he'd be getting his first paycheck.

But he'd been so concerned with getting a drink of water, he never bothered to ask! He didn't even know how much he was going to get paid.

He really didn't sleep much that night. He had to leave the house by seven in the morning to get to the mill, which was a good forty-five minute walk away. He remembered the words of the man in blue; he did not want to be late.

When he got there, the office wasn't open yet, but there were people showing up to start work at eight, mostly men in the same type of work clothes he saw the janitor – if he *was* the janitor – wearing the day before. There were also some women, mostly chubby girls in their early twenties, wearing dresses made of cloth that seemed to have had previous incarnations – maybe they had been tablecloths, pillow cases, laundry sacks … or even their brother's old Army duds. He figured it would be safe to follow them in. He got as far as a flight of steps when he ran into the man in blue.

"Where the hell you heading?" the man said. "You gotta go to the office first!"

"I know, but the door's locked."

"Oh, for Christ's sake!" the man said. "I forgot they don't open yet. God-damned it! C'mon, follow me."

The man took him through one door, past a stack of boxes with "Blake" stamped on them, down a dark hallway, and through another door that led into the office … it was the same door through which the man had exited the day before.

"Wait here for Martha," the man said. "She'll tell you what paperwork you gotta do. Then, see if you can figure out how to get back up to the third floor … that's where you were headed when you were followin' all those other workers. When you get there, go to the middle of the floor, and you'll see my desk. Meet me there."

He nodded. The man started back out the door, then turned.

"Oh, damn!" the man said. "Forgot to mention. My name's Artie. I'm the foreman."

The new employee sat in the office for a few more minutes until Martha showed up. He expected she would be the woman to whom he'd spoken the day before, but Martha turned out to be a woman in her sixties, as wide as she was short, with bluish-hair, thick glasses, and heavy black shoes.

"Good morning!" she said. "I believe we have some paperwork to do!"

He nodded, and for the next half-hour, he and Martha plowed through the paperwork required for a seventeen-year-old to work at the mill. He had working papers with him; his father had made him get them several months earlier, just in case he ever got a job. With all his documents in order, Martha sent him on his way, with directions to get to something called the throwing mill floor.

• • •

For the rest of that summer, he worked on that floor, first as a general bobbin boy, using a stick and some sandpaper to remove excess yarn from used bobbins. The job was monotonous, and, as had been implied, most of his colleagues were ... well, they were pretty much dimwits.

One who wasn't a dimwit was a fellow named George. He was in his early twenties, and he seemed to think he was too good to be working in the mill at all, much less at what was essentially its lowest level.

George spent a good part of the summer pointing out how his bobbin-boy colleagues were doing things wrong. George seemed to have only one friend in the mill – a phlegmatic young woman, about the same age, with a face like that of a dysenteric parrot. She worked on one of the machines, but she seemed to spend a good portion of her time trying to be Artie's sycophant. The consensus around the rest of the mill was that they were a good match, and the bobbin boy got the impression that if Artie ever left the mill, she would, too.

Each had a personality seemingly centered on running down everybody else, and neither was likely to draw much attention from the opposite sex. The young woman – Maggie was her name – didn't seem very attractive, at least to a seventeen-year-old boy. George had a ruddy, bulbous face, and despite his relatively young age, he already had a gut to rival any of those the boy had seen on the men staggering out of the corner saloon in his neighborhood.

The new bobbin boy spent most of the summer fending off the attempts of George and Maggie to demonize, demoralize and disturb him. They seemed to enjoy doing that to him and every other person in the plant they considered beneath them.

But he made enough pocket money to get his own portable record player, and to spend more time than he had before hanging out at one of the town's pizza parlors. Come August, he left the mill to return to school. Artie tried to talk him into keep working after school, but the boy wasn't all that interested. He figured he'd had enough of George and Maggie for one lifetime, and he'd already made up his mind that once he got out of high school, he was going to go right into the Army.

On the day he walked out of the mill in 1948, he practically ran home. He was glad he wasn't going to have to get up early to get to work anymore – although he'd be getting up much earlier, he found out, in the Army.

But as far as getting up to work in the mill, George and Maggie could do that until they dropped dead, as far as he was concerned. He figured he would move on to bigger and better things … and never go near that mill again!

2: YOU'RE IN THE MILL BIZ NOW

"H*oly Cow! The Giants won again!"*

In the very late summer of 1951, the amazing National League pennant race between the Brooklyn Dodgers and New York Giants had baseball fans all over the country excited.

For a now-twenty-year-old Giants fan fresh from a stint making coffee for sergeants and doing other essential military tasks in Korea, a good pennant race in September was just the way to celebrate his return home.

A few years in the Army had made him more sure of himself than he had been in 1948, but there was still something about knocking on doors and looking for jobs that didn't work quite well for him. He still had no interest in working with his father in the garage, and while his time in the service had helped him mature quite a bit, he still didn't have anything close to a marketable skill. They weren't looking for coffee makers, soup ladlers, or latrine-scrubbers back in the coal-town-turned-factory-town where he was born.

If he'd had a resume, the only two things on it would have been his Army record and that summer he'd spent working as a bobbin boy at the Blake Silk Mill. Granted, his time in the Army had given him some of that walking-around money he'd lacked in 1948. But he still needed a steady job if he wanted to get a car, and to maybe even move out of his parents' house in a few months.

He was a veteran, but in many ways, he was still a boy. He spent about two weeks looking for work, but couldn't find any. He walked back up and down the hills again, past the ribbons of houses on which the paint had started to peel just a bit more.

And so, one morning, he trudged up the hill to the place where he'd spent that summer cleaning bobbins, and watching George and Maggie try to bully their way to the top. There wasn't much else he could do; he walked up the hill to see if he could become one of the boys again. A bobbin boy.

He walked into the same office into which he'd walked those summers before, and he didn't recognize the women there. The old ones had been replaced, voluntarily or otherwise. So as he had done a few years before, he just asked this 1951 receptionist for a job application, and she handed him one on a clipboard, with a pencil on a string tied to it.

Except for filling in that he'd worked at Blake in the summer of 1948, and his affirmative answer to whether he was a veteran, the responses were virtually identical to the ones he'd given back then. He gave the application to the woman, who took it and looked it over.

"Oh, so you've worked here before?" she said. "Let me see if they want to talk to you now."

She took the application to a man he seemed to remember from his previous stint at the mill; the man was some sort of big deal with the company, the type of office-dwelling fellow you might never meet if you spent thirty years working on the mill floor. That man looked it over, and then two other men entered the office from the door that led to and from the mill floor.

He immediately recognized Artie; except for a few extra pounds around the waistline, the foreman hadn't changed much. Artie looked at the application, nodded his head, looked out to the waiting room and waved to the former bobbin boy, who returned the wave.

The other man was in his forties, and he was wearing what looked to be a white laboratory coat. And that wasn't the only thing that made this man different. This man had an air about him that he had never seen anywhere in this building before. He was used to the guys in the blue work clothes, or the fellows in the white, short-sleeved Manhattan shirts. But what was a man in a lab coat doing at Blake Silk Mill? And talking to Artie, no less?

The three men began talking. The former bobbin boy couldn't hear what they were saying, but he could tell from the body language of the three men that the fellow in the lab coat was … well, he was *pissed off*!

The receptionist could hear it all, though:

"Artie, this guy just dropped off this application," said the big deal. "You know him?"

"Yeah," said Artie. "Worked here one summer. Bobbin boy. Lemme see …"

Artie looked over the application.

"Hey … he's a vet now!"

The man in the lab coat tugged at his tie, his expression tightening.

"Well, we don't really need nobody right now," Artie said.

The man in the lab arched his eyebrows, his face getting red.

"Don't keep up with that shit, Artie!" the man in the lab coat said. "You keep pulling that on me when you know …"

"Now just a minute!" said the big deal. He tried to put his arm on the man in the lab coat, but the man just brushed it aside.

"You two oughta know that you don't wanna keep pushing me!"

Artie and the big deal seemed flustered. The man in the lab coat pointed out toward the hallway, where he got his first look at the former bobbin boy.

It looked like something out of the Army, with a couple of smarmy captains about to get reamed out by a big-shot colonel.

"I've been coming out here for six months now, and I've been telling all of you what needs to be done around here," the man in the lab coat said.

"But I can't keep coming out here! I have other assignments, other places to go. I've been telling you all this time that I need to train somebody to do what I do ... I don't know what else I have to do to get through to all of you!"

Artie rubbed his forehead while the big deal put his hand to his mouth.

"You two ... all of the so-called big shots around here ... you all know that I can have this place shut down, don't you?" the man in the lab coat continued. "You want hundreds of people out of work? You want that in the newspapers?"

Artie turned as if he had no reply. The big deal just shrugged. The man in the lab coat went on:

"You know I can't hang around Blake forever. I need somebody to teach this job to. If I can't teach somebody here to do it, then ... well, listen ... If I can't get somebody to teach this job to, then it won't be long before Blake is the laughing stock of this industry. You'll never keep up with all the changes, and you'll be out of business so fast you won't know what hit you. You think you can go on forever the way you have been? There are a lot of people out there who would be glad to take every scrap of business you have ... and they will all have people doing the same job as me. And you won't have anybody!"

The man in the lab coat turned and looked back out toward the hallway. He pointed at the one-time bobbin boy.

"You see that kid out there? I could train that kid to do this job, and in a couple of weeks, before you guys knew what was happening, that kid would know more about the operation here than the two of you put together. You'd be crawling on your knees asking that kid what to do next!"

Artie and the big deal looked at each other.

"That kid?" Artie said. "I don't know ... I was thinkin' about that fellow George?"

"George???" the man in the lab coat bellowed. "You mean that brown-nosing punk you sent up a couple of weeks ago? I wouldn't let him open a soda bottle in my room, much less work with any of the stuff I have up there. You want this place going up in smoke like Hiroshima? No, keep that jerk-off away from me."

The big deal wrote something on his note pad. The man in the lab coat pointed at the bobbin boy again.

"No, let's use that kid! You said he worked here before, right? You said he's a vet? He's gotta have some smarts, doesn't he? I want you two to bring that kid in, give him a job for a while, and then once I'm ready in a week or two, I'll start breaking him in, training him to take over for me."

Artie nodded his head. The big deal whispered something to Artie, turned and walked away.

"Okay!" Artie said. "We'll let him go back to the bobbins for a week, and then … well, if he's still here … he's all yours!"

"Good deal!" said the man in the lab coat, who then followed the big deal out of the office.

On the other side of the glass, the bobbin boy couldn't hear any of this, and he wondered if he should leave. He started to go toward the door when he noticed Artie rushing out toward the hallway.

"Hey kid!" Artie said as he emerged through the door. "Where ya headed?"

"Just gonna go home," he said. "I figured you guys didn't remember me."

"Sure we do!" Artie said. "We was just talkin' about you in there! Been overseas, eh?"

"Yeah," he said. "But now I kinda need a job!"

"Well," Artie said, "I can't offer much … things been kinda slow here, ya know? But we … we could bring you back for your old job … at least to start."

"You mean … to be a bobbin boy?"

"Yeah."

He thought about it for a moment. Had he spent that time in Korea to come back here and be a bobbin boy again? Not really. But nobody else was offering him a job. And at least he knew how to do this one.

He wondered if George and Maggie were still up there. He didn't relish the thought of dealing with them again. On the other hand, he was older, maybe wiser, now. He figured he could handle whatever they tried to pull.

And then he thought of the man in the lab coat. He wondered what the deal was with him.

So he nodded and shook Artie's hand, sealing the deal.

"Be here six o'clock tomorrow morning," Artie said. "You know the drill."

He nodded and smiled. He started to leave, but then turned as Artie was going back into the office.

"Hey Artie?" he said.

"Yeah?"

"That fellow in the white coat."

"What about him?"

"Uh … nothing. Just wondering who he was."

Artie's face turned red.

"Him?" he said. "He … he's the chemist!"

3: THE CHEMIST

It was possible for a relatively observant person to work, oh, thirty years or so at the Blake Silk Mill without really knowing much about what the company actually did.

The mill's main function was to refine raw textiles into a marketable product – yarns, threads, things like that.

The people who worked on the throwing machines – they made up more than half the mill's workforce – only knew what was in front of them. They knew when to check the row after row of bobbins to see when they were empty, and knew when to replenish the supply. But they really didn't know much about how the textiles were treated – that is, what was done to them chemically at the mill.

And most of the other workers at the mill had jobs relating to packaging, shipping, or stocking the raw materials needed for the entire process. About a dozen or so workers toiled in a hot, steamy part of the plant, and they had something to do with the way the materials were treated. But none of them really knew anything about the science behind it all. Neither did most of the supervisors, such as Artie.

And then there were the bobbin boys and their adult contemporaries, whose world was limited to scraping unused thread off the metal or wooden bobbins – larger versions of the spools found in their mothers' old sewing baskets, really – and perhaps wiping some oil off them. They knew the least about the whole operation, and were more likely to be handed a broom and told to sweep up the floors than they were to find out anything about the inner workings of textile science.

At Blake, and at virtually every other postwar American textile mill, that knowledge was limited to one man, a man who spent most of his time on the top floor of the mill, but whose presence in any other part of the operation could bring it all to a halt, just on his word.

Nobody at Blake had ever seen him when he wasn't wearing his white lab coat. Actually, more than half the workers at Blake had never seen him *at all.* Most of them didn't even know he was there.

He looked to be in his early thirties, tall, skinny, with a slightly receding hairline and glasses that he took off and held in his right hand when somebody got under his skin. Whenever he came down from his domain upstairs, or was in any part of the plant other than his own area, he always had a wooden clipboard in his left hand. He'd never actually struck anybody with it, but there were times when it seemed as if he might.

Actually, he wasn't even an employee of Blake itself. He worked for a major chemical company based in New York, and he was sent to various textile mills under contract, with more or less free rein to oversee operations. At times, he could be found at one of the other textile mills in town – and, in fact, elsewhere in the state.

He graduated from a technical school in Philadelphia a few months after Pearl Harbor, and then went right into the Army during the war, specializing first in textiles and then as a general chemist. There was a rumor among those at Blake who knew of his presence that he'd had a hand in developing lightweight flak jackets for Allied pilots during the war. For all anybody at Blake knew, though, he might have single-handedly brought the Germans and Japanese to their knees in 1945.

After the war, he got a job with a chemical company in New York, and began working as a consultant to his first love – the commercial textile industry. His first few years were spent in New England, where the textile industry was then a major part of the regional economy. After bouncing around places such as New Bedford and Narrangasset, he was assigned to another region, and spent his time in upstate New York and Eastern Pennsylvania.

He didn't approach an assignment at a new mill as if he was better than the workers there; in fact, he seemed to have quite a bit of respect for those working on the machines. In particular, he seemed to have great concern for the welfare of those who were considered to dwell on the bottom of the mill totem pole – the stock boys, maintenance workers, and, of course, the bobbin boys. Occasionally, he would stop and talk to them, or even offer to buy them a drink out of one of the vending machines.

But he had a different opinion of the people who ran and managed the mills. *They* were the ones who got under his skin. From his perspective, the managers thought they were better than their workers when, as far as he was concerned, they were easily replaceable. He especially disliked two people at Blake – and their names were George and Maggie.

In the years during which the bobbin boy had been in the service, George and Maggie had moved into management positions, of a sort, at Blake. George was an assistant foreman – he reported to Artie, but George figured it was only a matter of time before he would have Artie's job. Maggie had risen to become an assistant floorlady, ostensibly helping out Flossie, who was the mill's main floorlady.

Flossie was, by nature, a sweet person, and was the one member of management even the chemist held in high regard. He even had flowers delivered to her on her birthday. But she was getting up in years, and so was Artie. Workers who planned to be around Blake for a while tried not to think about the foreboding prospect of George and Maggie taking over those jobs.

But the chemist wasn't planning to be at Blake much longer. His company's contract with the mill's management was running out in a few months, and he'd pretty much had his fill of the place. He wasn't concerned about George and Maggie – in fact, he almost relished the prospect of knocking them down a few pegs when they moved up in mill status. But he knew that if he didn't train somebody to do his job, his company might just want him to hang around Blake indefinitely, and he hardly wanted to spend a few more years working on the top floor of a stone building in the middle of nowhere.

So for at least a month, he had been harassing upper management at Blake, trying to get them to hire somebody he could train to take over for him permanently. His original idea was to hire somebody from his alma mater, a young, aspiring chemist, as he himself had been before the war.

But while he had considerable influence at Blake, he couldn't just snap his fingers and get the company – particularly the family members whose name was on the building – to make a spot for a college-boy chemist.

One day, realizing he wasn't going to get his college graduate, he decided to try to persuade management to give him a protégé by insisting that they bring somebody up from the mill floor, a young, smart fellow he could train, somebody to whom he could teach the scientific secrets of the mill practically from scratch.

Artie's preference was that the chemist would take George off his hands – he wasn't any more of a fan of the red-faced striver than anybody else – but each attempt at that was rebuffed with a vengeance.

On the other hand, when he noticed that boyish veteran standing on the other side of the window, the chemist thought he saw a prospect – and perhaps saw something of himself. He thought of his own wartime experience, then how he got his job fresh out of technical school. This kid had been to war and back. And these pompous clowns were going to make him grovel to them? Make him be … a bobbin boy?

No they weren't! Not with the chemist around!

So after the argument in the office, in which of course, the chemist prevailed, it was determined that they would give the kid a job – his old job, in fact. And after he made it through a week or so, and hadn't quit or caused any trouble, they would turn him over to the man on the top floor.

But the kid didn't know that. And what if he didn't want to be turned over?

4: "EIGHT-TWO-ONE-FIVE"

The bobbin boy's first week back on the floor was not an easy one. George and Maggie acted as if they didn't know who he was, but he knew they remembered him. Maggie in particular had become quite obnoxious in her new post, treating him, and virtually every worker under her influence, as if they were the lowest of the low.

Granted, some of the bobbin boys were of very limited intelligence. The job they had was about the only one they could get, much less keep. To Maggie, they were idiots, morons she could boss around – and she often told them that to their faces!

Whereas an experienced machine operator might let her ramblings go in one ear and out the other, or might respond with a sneer, the bobbin boys were almost too easy to push around. She rode them mercilessly.

George, meanwhile, walked around seemingly not doing much of anything. George had the air of a European nobleman to whom rank and privilege had been restored after a bloody revolution. It was as if he thought he owned the place. Most of the time, he couldn't be bothered talking to bobbin boys, but on one occasion, he did walk by, blurted out something about there being too much oil on one of the bobbins, and walked away.

After a rough first week on the floor, the bobbin boy spent a good part of his first weekend off at a corner bar with some of his friends, wondering how much longer he could handle the job. He did not feel like returning on Monday, and on Sunday night, he promised himself to walk out the next day – at least if things did not improve by lunchtime.

After about two-and-a-half hours of scraping and wiping, stacking and piling, he had pretty much decided things weren't going to improve. He wanted to walk out before lunch, but he figured he'd stick it out at least until then, if only to prove to himself that he had *some* self-discipline.

About a half-hour before lunch, he heard some people mumbling behind him. He turned to see Maggie storming off in a huff, George grimacing, Artie appearing indifferent, and the man in the lab coat, smiling but serious, coming toward him, clipboard in one hand, and the other one extended. His smile displayed yet another victory over his nemeses.

"Floyd?" he said, marking the first time that anybody at Blake had ever called the bobbin boy by his first name.

"Uh … you mean me?"

"Yes, you. How are you? They keeping you busy with all this important work down here?"

"Well … it's … it's okay, I guess."

The man in the lab coat put his free hand on the bobbin boy's shoulder. "Now don't try to give *me* any of that! This job, and some of the people down here … they are *anything* but okay!"

They both smiled. The bobbin boy wasn't sure what to say or do. He knew this guy was pretty important. He wondered why he had been approached by him.

The other bobbin boys, bent over and scraping and wiping, glanced at them with surprise, seemingly puzzled by the fact that anybody so important would pay attention to any of them.

Artie, leaning against the foreman's desk, was listening. George was pacing around, just as Maggie had found a machine operator on whom to take out her frustrations – at least until Flossie intervened and sent Maggie away to harass some other poor soul.

"Listen, you have lunch in, what, a half-hour?" the man in the lab coat said.

"Uh … yeah."

"Okay, you finish up here and go to lunch. Don't leave anything here though – you know, none of your personal items. After lunch, you're not to come back here …"

"But …" the bobbin boy said, pointing at Artie.

"Don't worry about anybody else. I said you don't have to come back here. That's all that matters. After lunch, you take the freight elevator upstairs. You need to punch in a special code to get up there …"

The man in the lab coat wrote a few numbers on his clipboard, then folded the paper, and handed it to the bobbin boy.

"… you come up there, and we'll talk about some things you're going to be doing around here … for me!"

He took the paper and put it in his pocket. Every Blake Silk Mill employee within eyesight of the two of them saw what had just happened. He wasn't sure whether they thought he was being promoted or fired. He didn't know the answer himself. Why did the man in the lab coat approach *him*? He had no idea, but he did know that the offer the man in the lab coat was making sounded a lot better than even another afternoon spent cleaning and scraping bobbins.

The lunch whistle blew about twenty-five minutes later. Even during his previous summer at Blake, the bobbin boy usually had eaten lunch pretty much by himself, on a small concrete stoop near the main entrance to the mill. A few other fellows sat out there at lunchtime, but they were older, and they almost never even looked at him, either that summer, or in the first week of his return engagement.

This time, though, he decided he really needed to be alone. He walked away from the building, past the main parking lot, to a small wooded area. About 20 feet into the wooded area, he found a large rock, where he sat down, took the ham sandwich his mother had made for him out of his paper bag, and thought about what had just happened.

What did it all mean? Was this guy a pervert or something? Did he take young guys up there and stick his beaker up their butts? Or was he an ax murderer? Did bobbin boys go up there and never come back? Did he have some sort of weird gas chamber up there, with a chute to drop the bodies down into a vat of acid? This guy ... I'd never even seen him the previous summer I was here! What made him such a big shot? And why had he taken such an interest in me?

The thoughts swirled. Maybe he should have stayed in the Army!

But he figured it couldn't hurt to go up and talk to the guy. Besides, everybody had seen their conversation. So if he went up there and never came back ... well, wouldn't *somebody* notice?

Then he remembered that after the man in the lab coat approached him, everybody looked kind of intimidated. He remembered how Artie and the big shot had cowered in the office. It was a good feeling, being on the other side of that. He liked intimidating George and Maggie, in particular.

So when it came time to go back inside, he took a deep breath, and when he got to the floor, rather than move on to the bobbin station about midway through the building, he detoured to the freight elevator, located just to the left of the employee entrance. `

He entered the elevator, a creaky, iron-and-wooden model that seemed out of another century, like something they had at the Tower of London. He took the paper out of his pocket. He looked at the code, then punched it in on the keypad next to the door.

"Eight-two-one-five"

The freight elevator moved as if it was being pushed by a couple of dying elephants. As it creaked upwards, he wondered what would happen if he got stuck. There was no phone, no apparent way to contact anybody. He figured he'd have to crawl around the cage and climb up to see the man in the lab coat.

Finally, the elevator crept to the top floor. It stopped with a jolt. He had to manually lift the cage-type doors open, using a belt that was attached to the top half. Then, using a lever, he opened the heavy iron doors that led to the top floor, a floor to which few others – not Artie, not Flossie, and certainly not Maggie – had ever ascended.

As the doors opened, he saw the man in the lab coat seated on a stool, writing on his clipboard.

"Well, well!" the man in the lab coat said with a smile upon seeing that his guest of honor had arrived. "Welcome to the world of chemistry!"

5: CALL ME 'THE TESTER'

The bobbin boy's first sensory exposure to the world of chemistry had not been the sight of the man in the lab coat, nor had it been the man's verbal exhortation.

Without a doubt, the first impression had been the odiferous wave of chemical fumes he noticed as soon as the door opened.

He was no stranger to odd smells, of course. His whole neighborhood had smelled of culm – the waste product of coal mining – for as long as he could remember. It was an indescribable sulphuric odor, pungent, noxious, one he swore must have been dug up from hell itself.

Not only that, but half of the children with whom he went to school for thirteen years had bathed only sporadically, if ever. So he knew all too well the scent of bad hygiene.

And in the Army, well, he'd been exposed to everything from a barracks full of perpetually farting Alabamans and Mississippians, to the aromatic mixture of urine, vomit and crap scooped up during latrine duty.

But this … this was different. It was almost sour and sweet at the same time. He had the feeling that it could burn your lungs in an instant, but he also could imagine that a fellow could become … well … almost *addicted* to it! He couldn't imagine that sucking it in eight hours a day, five days a week, fifty-two weeks a year could be *good* for a person, but he also had that postwar confidence that if American industry exposed you to it … well … *they* must know what *they're* doing!

On his way up on the elevator, he had visualized the man in his white lab coat, with his omnipresent clipboard, working in a serene, almost sterile environment. Instead, he found him ensconced in a world of vats and jugs, ladles, spoons, and prongs. Everything seemed stained, corroded, or tainted. He wondered what it might take to set the whole thing off and launch Blake Silk Mill into outer space!

"So, in case they didn't tell you, I am the *chemist,*" the man in the lab coat said, forever changing the bobbin boy's perception of this now-mystical mill figure. "Take a good look. Nobody gets to come up here, you know? Even old man Blake … he's never been up here. Roberts … you know, the superintendent, the guy I was talking to in the office last week … he came up here once and ended up down in the men's room puking his guts out."

He gently tapped the bobbin boy on the chest.

"You know that cocksucker George down there? That kiss-ass who thinks he runs the place? He thinks he should have a say in what goes on up here. I'd like to get him up here and stick his head in a vat for a few seconds … I'd go to jail, but he'd end up looking like the 'Phantom of the Opera!' "

The chemist! You had to like his way of thinking!

"Okay, let me fill you in on what I'm looking at here," the chemist said. "First off, I bet you wonder what I do up here."

The bobbin boy nodded. He kept looking around for that chute, or a beaker.

"You and everybody else, that is … for now, anyway," the chemist said. "Simply put, though, I am in charge of the most important part of the operation here. For all the work that goes on downstairs, for all the noise and commotion, for all the heavy machinery … if we did not chemically treat the textiles that come through here, there would be no reason for us to be here …

The chemist smirked as he edited himself.

"Well, I should say, for 'Blake' to be here. I don't actually work for Blake, you know."

"I didn't know that!"

"No, I work for a company in New York called Towers Chemical. You know the password I gave you to get up here?"

"Yes," the boy said, looking at the paper. "Eight ... two ... one ... five."

"That's right," the chemist said. "It's based on a complicated chemical formula that none of the other knuckleheads in this building can comprehend. Let me explain it to you."

He walked up to a blackboard on the wall.

"Eight ... What's the eighth letter in the alphabet?"

The bobbin boy counted them out on his fingers.

"H!"

"Good. Now, let's add a 'two,' just for the hell of it. So you have 'H' and 'Two.' Correct?"

The boy nodded.

"Now, what is the fifteenth letter of the alphabet?"

He counted them out again.

"O?"

"That's right! So you have "H," "Two," and "O. You know what that stands for?"

"I think so," the bobbin boy said. "Isn't that the ... isn't that what water is made of?"

"That's right!" the chemist boomed. "Eight-two-one-five! H2O! It's the chemical designation for ... water! That's the code to get up here. None of this stuff ... see all these vats and jugs? None of them are worth a damn without ..."

"Water?"

"Absolutely! Water! And the geniuses downstairs, from Blake to your bobbin boy buddies, they aren't clever enough to figure out that the code to get up here is ... *water*!"

The bobbin boy smiled. He couldn't help but like this fellow! Compared to everybody he'd met at the mill, especially the managers, he seemed so ... *so human*! He knew he'd made a good decision to take him up on his offer ... and there wasn't a chute in sight!

"Now listen, Floyd," the chemist said. "The reason I had you come up here ... and I picked you over that cocksucker I just mentioned, and over every other dickstain down there ... is that, like I said, I don't work for Blake. And I don't particularly feel like spending the rest of my life in this attic, and in this big stone building, and in this town ... no offense, but I just don't want to.

"So I tried to get them to hire a kid from the school I went to in Philadelphia, the textile college there. But I couldn't get them to open their God-damned wallets for that. So the next step, I figured, was to get them to send me somebody who was already here.

"So I talked to Artie ... you know Artie, right?"

The bobbin boy nodded.

"Artie wanted to send me that cocksucker George. I told them where they could stick that idea ... like I said, he isn't getting anywhere near any of this.

"As it turned out, though, you walked in right when I was arguing with them about it. They said that you'd worked here before, and that you'd been in the Army. I liked that."

"Are you a vet?"

"Well, you could say that. I didn't see any combat or anything, but I was ... well, let me tell you ... actually ... I *still* can't really go into too much detail about what I did during the war. But yeah, I was in the Army. In fact, I was an officer. Made it to major by the end of the war. They even wanted me to stay in and work at the Pentagon, work on all these different kinds of explosives they want to use to drop from big bombers and all. Some of the things they're working on, Floyd … God help us if we ever really use it!

"But I'd had enough of that stuff. I wanted to get into commercial textiles, you know? That's what I was trained for."

The bobbin boy nodded and offered a playful salute, which the chemist returned.

"You were in Korea, right?"

"Yeah, for a year or so," he said. "We were mostly support. I think I made more pots of coffee for the sergeants than I did fire any rounds. But it was a good experience."

"Well, I figured that anybody who went over there at your age, and did all that, had what it takes to take on a big job here. So I asked … well, I didn't *ask*, I mostly *told* them that you were coming up here."

The bobbin boy rubbed his chin. Earlier, he was hesitant to ask any questions, but he felt more at ease now.

"Can I ask you something?" he said.

"Sure."

"How come you got so much authority around here? I never seen all those guys snap to it like they do around you."

The chemist smiled, tapped him on the shoulder, and for the first time since the boy had first seen him, he put down his clipboard, placing it on a table near the elevator.

"Here's the thing, Floyd," he said. "Before the company sent me here, this place had things all fucked up chemically. The stuff they were sending out was … well, it was crap. Substandard shit, the kind of stuff you'd get from some jerkwater Asian country. They were scared they were going to go out of business. They knew they had to get their systems straightened out, or they were going under. I guess they were desperate, so they called our company and they sent me here to see what the problem was.

"Well, it didn't take me long. This operation up here, it was like something out of an old movie. They tried doing the chemistry themselves with some assholes they sent up here just to get them off the floor downstairs.

It's a miracle they didn't blow the place up. I spent the first six months here cleaning this place up … as crazy as it might look to you now, it looked a hundred times worse when I got here.

"The biggest thing is, they had no program. If they needed to adjust their chemistry, they'd call somebody from some other mill. That person would give them their formulas, but they were half-assed to begin with, and then these assholes here would mix them wrong. They'd end up with half the product oversaturated, and half of it missing all the treatments.

"But the absolute biggest problem was testing."

"Testing?"

"Yeah, testing. They just would run the chemicals through the pipes and into the machinery, but nobody was going down there and testing to see how the chemicals were being distributed. Were they being mixed properly? How were they reacting when they were exposed to the air, or to the textiles themselves? Were there any blockages? Was there too much water, or not enough?"

"Sounds like a lot of work."

"It is, but the key is consistency and accuracy. I know these chemicals like the back of my hand. The idiots they had in here before couldn't figure out the difference between piss and water, never mind these volatile chemicals! And they never … I mean *never* … they never did any testing!"

The bobbin boy noticed how much emphasis the chemist put on testing. He wondered where this was leading.

"So here's the thing," the chemist said. "If you're interested, I'd like to have you work up here with me for, well, at least six months, maybe a year. Of course, you don't have the education to become a full-blown chemist – pardon the pun!"

They both laughed.

"But you don't need that here. All they need here is somebody with half a brain who understands the importance of what I just said. So I'd like to leave here and put you in charge of all this. My idea … now let me know if you think this is something you'd be interested in ... is to create a new position of sorts. I'd like for this place to have ... *a tester*!"

How the world works! When the bobbin boy arrived for work that morning, he didn't even know the man in the lab coat *was* the chemist. Now, a few hours later, he felt as if he was in the presence of some sort of one-man, textile-industry Round Table, and that he was being proposed for a knighthood. As a *tester*!

"Uh ... you mean *me*?" he said.

The chemist smiled and nodded.

"Yes ... *You!*"

And with that, the bobbin boy spent the rest of the day on the top floor, but he didn't learn anything about chemistry that first day. The chemist told him about his days in the Army, and about how he was hoping to get married pretty soon, to a girlfriend he had in New York.

They talked about the bobbin boy's ambitions, about how so many of his friends really didn't have too many prospects for a good job, and how he would like to get some money together, mainly to get himself a car.

"So, let's just get this straight," the chemist said. "You're on board with this?"

Floyd, the bobbin boy, nodded his head. And from that moment, Floyd was no longer the bobbin boy. He was the tester-in-waiting, the heir to this strangely aromatic domain, the crown prince of chemistry, the soon-to-be lord of the special manor waiting atop the Blake Silk Mill freight elevator.

"Yeah," he said. "I'd like to learn all this."

So the chemist opened the iron doors, and then the cage, and rode the elevator down with Floyd – no code was required for the downward trip – to the mill floor.

Then the chemist took him in to see a few management types. They stopped by to break the news to Artie – he seemed not to care that much – and Flossie – who wished Floyd well – and then the two of them punched in the mysterious code and rode back upstairs. The next morning, Floyd started to learn the chemical mysteries that would turn him into a tester.

Over the next few months, Floyd often had to venture down to the mill floor with jugs of chemicals. Eventually, before the chemist returned to New York for good, he taught Floyd how to test the machinery in the mill for all the issues to which he had referred on that first afternoon.

But before the chemist left, Floyd had several encounters with George and Maggie on the floor. Every time George gave him a dirty look, Floyd thought of the chemist's wish to turn George into a disfigured figure from a Gaston Leroux novel.

And if Maggie looked at him the wrong way, Floyd just smiled. He knew that pissed her off more than anything.

George and Maggie were seething that this kid – *this bobbin boy!* – seemed to be on the fast track to becoming a Blake Silk Mill untouchable. They growled that their own machinations had gotten them no higher than supervising a few dozen cretins on the floor, while this guy seemingly had written his ticket to the top – or had it written *for* him by that damned, white-coated chemist!

The first few times Floyd came downstairs with the jugs, each of them tried to find fault with something he did – maybe he left a stain on the floor, or he didn't have an apron on, or he bumped a rack of empty bobbins on his way back to the elevator.

They whined to Artie and to Flossie. Maggie pestered as many higher-ups as she could about it. George even drafted a memo he was going to send to Old Man Blake.

But, without fail, it was as if the chemist knew what they were going to do before they did it. Any time they even thought about giving Floyd a hard time, one or both of them got called into the office before Floyd even knew anything about it. They got their respective butts chewed out so often that they felt as if higher management's teeth marks were embedded in their rear-ends.

By the time the chemist went home to New York and Floyd had been elevated to tester, George and Maggie, along with everybody else at Blake, knew that this lowly bobbin boy had undoubtedly become an untouchable. He had been handed the baton of power that had belonged to the chemist, and his upstairs domain was like a quiet Forbidden City atop the drone of the mechanized drudgery below.

Yes, the bobbin boy who once was the lowest of the low was now essential to the mill's entire operation – and best of all, only he, and the mysterious, departed chemist, really knew why!

So he would, of course, enjoy total autonomy in the world of Blake Silk Mill.

As would anybody else on whom his favor might someday rest.

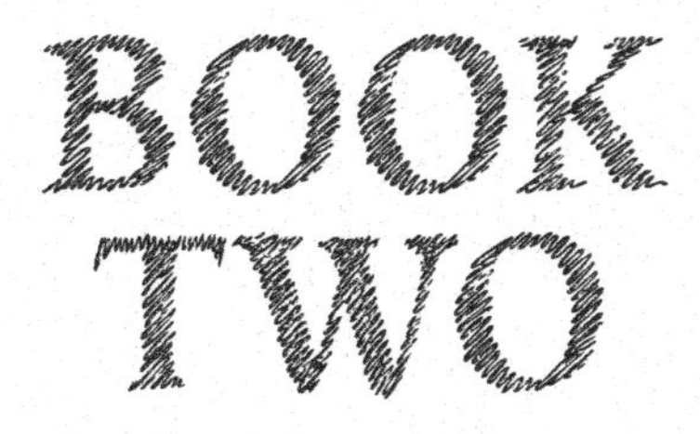
BOOK
TWO

6: A SUMMER JOB

The first thing Chris Tiller did when he got to North Side High School on the morning of May 27, 1971 was to head straight to the office to ask what he had to do to get his working papers.

He was now sixteen years old, officially old enough to get a real job – no mowing lawns or delivering newspapers. All he needed was to get those papers and he could start looking for work at some of the factories that were still scattered around the town.

"Yes young man, may I help you?" said the woman behind the main desk in the office.

"Um … who do I talk to so I can get my working papers?"

The woman, one of the many dowdy, middle-aged women who seemingly had been working at this school since its cornerstone was laid seventy years before, put a pencil to her mouth and thought.

"Well," she said. "Do you have a job lined up?"

Chris shook his head that he did not.

"You have to have a job lined up in order to get working papers," the woman said. "But I will tell you that really you don't have to work at that particular place to get them. All you really need is to have somebody at a potential employer sign the form, and then you can work wherever you want, really."

"Okay," Chris said. "Can I have the form then?"

"*May I*?" said the woman, sounding an awful lot like the English teacher Chris figured she would have preferred to be. "May I have the form?"

"May I?" he said grudgingly.

The woman came close to smiling, and then handed Chris a small yellow form.

"You fill out this information here … you know, your name, address, and all that," she said. "Then you take it to your prospective employer, and they will fill it out down here. Then you bring it back to us and we give you your working papers."

Chris nodded and wandered out of the office. As he headed off for the ten-minute walk to his house along the cracked and pockmarked sidewalks, he looked around at the dreary buildings he passed daily: a rundown, smelly flophouse that dared to put the word "Hotel" in its title; a grungy Lithuanian Club that emitted the aroma of flat beer twenty-four hours a day; and a gas station with two tanks, a grimy office with a peanut-dispensing machine in it, and a German Shepherd tied up inside that looked as if it would devour the leg of the next person who walked in.

He crossed a rust-infected railroad bridge along generally rotting wood railroad ties, and walked a block or so up an unpaved back street until he got to his house. His mother was home, but he didn't feel like going inside, so he sat on the back porch, thinking.

Chris did not want to spend the rest of his life in this town, and he certainly did not want to spend it working in some factory. He wanted to go to college and learn about television production.

He and his friends used to play basketball on outside courts that were next to a local junior high school whose basement actually hosted the studio of one of the town's television stations.

On occasion, and in between games, some of the kids used to sneak into the school and head down to the basement, where the television station had some vending machines. If you showed up around six in the evening, you could even see them doing the local news in there.

It was a pretty slipshod operation, but Chris was enchanted by all the gadgets and gimmickry. He thought maybe he could go to school and become a cameraman or something – he knew he would never be one of the guys who went on the air!

But he knew that he had to work over the next couple of summers, at least, to even think about being able to afford to go to college. His parents didn't have any spare money. He was the last of five kids. Only one had gone to college, and the other three were all married and gone already. He was the only one left, but the cost of raising the previous four had tapped out his parents. He was going to have to pay for at least part of the cost.

Not only didn't Chris want to work in a factory when he was older; he didn't want to work in one at all, even for a summer job! He would have preferred to work, say, in a fast-food joint, or would have even washed dishes in a diner. But he and his friends had been rebuffed at every turn when they sought out those jobs.

One night, he was in a basketball game with some guys he knew from school, including one or two who were really good players. A few of them started talking about what they were going to do over the summer, and Chris heard one guy say that he knew of at least one place where they hired kids who hadn't had a job before.

He thought he knew where the place was. It was about a half-hour walk from his house, in the opposite direction from school. It was up on a hill. From what he'd heard, they'd hired a couple of other guys from his school the previous summer.

So Chris Tiller took the working papers form from his pocket and decided that the next morning, he would make that walk up that hill, and see if they would at least sign the form for him. And maybe they'd even give him a job.

He would walk up to the Blake Silk Mill.

• • •

It was a warm, late-May morning when he started heading toward the mill. The route was a familiar one; he'd taken it several times to go watch ballgames at a nearby field.

It took him through an old freight yard, past a few bums he'd seen for years. One of them walked around carrying a shopping bag, constantly ducking something – Japanese Zeros, enraged seagulls, who knew?

After that, he strolled past blocks and blocks of tire places, small garages, a diner or two, and then about a quarter-mile of used car dealerships. It was the city's strip of fast-talkers, men who would have you in an old Fury or Rambler before you knew what hit you. His father never owned a new car, so he was all too familiar with the routine both seller and buyer went through at these used-car joints.

Eventually, he turned a corner and passed several blocks of small houses, all of them just like his. They were made of wood, crammed together like boxes of Jell-O on a grocer's shelves. Each had a creaky front porch, and many of them had old-timers sitting on those porches.

He had a feeling those folks had been sitting on those porches through wars, assassinations, the whole nine yards. And they probably never noticed most of it.

Making another turn, he saw the hill. The street rose at least thirty degrees upward, which for a healthy teenager presented no physical challenge. However, he had the sense that the hill was there as an obstacle, that he had to climb this hill if he wanted to have even a chance to get his papers signed and his job prospects boosted.

So he did it, and the next thing he knew, the big building rose up to his right. He saw the weather-beaten brass sign next to the office door:

"Blake Textiles, Inc."

He'd always heard this place, and the others like it in town, referred to as "silk mills." He glanced at the sign, and noted that the word "Blake" seemed a bit more faded than the rest of the words. Upon closer examination, he could see that the words "Silk Mill" had been covered over with a metal plate to make room for the current nomenclature.

He opened the door and went inside, standing in the hallway, and he saw hard-boiled old offices that looked as if Sam Spade might be somewhere inside. He waited for someone on the other end of the glass to acknowledge his presence. A woman in her late fifties slowly waddled over, and she opened the glass with a discouraged look on her face.

"May I help you?" she said.

"Uh … yes … I was wondering, is this where I would go to … uh … fill out a job application?"

"Summer work?" she said.

"Uh … yeah."

The woman sighed and picked up a clipboard with a pencil tied to it. She handed it to Chris and told him to fill out the application.

He sat down and plodded through the application. He had trouble coming up with three references, but he finally settled on his parish priest, his doctor, and a friend he knew. He didn't know their addresses or phone numbers, but he remembered that one of his brothers once told him nobody ever checked those anyway.

"Here you go," he said as he handed the clipboard back to the woman. "I … I also need to have my working papers filled out."

"Working papers?" she said with a grimace.

"Well, not the papers … just the form. I need to have them filled out … you know … so I can …"

"All right then!" she said. "I'll give them to the superintendent. Wait here."

A few minutes later, a portly, gray-haired man wandered out of the office. Chris figured he was in his late fifties, but in truth, the man hadn't even seen fifty yet. His expression suggested that he was irritated at having to stop whatever he was doing, and when he crossed through the door into the hallway, he growled at his younger visitor.

"So, are you … Tiller?" he said.

Chris got up, nodded his head, and extended his hand, which the older man shook with little enthusiasm.

"You got working papers to sign?"

"Well, not the papers … you know, the form?"

"Yeah, yeah, the form," the man said. "Well, let's see it."

Chris took the form out and showed it to the man, who examined it as if he was a brain surgeon studying an X-ray. In truth, if he'd seen one of these forms, he'd seen a hundred. But he usually signed them, knowing that most of the teenagers would never set foot in the mill again anyway.

"So, you lookin' for summer work?" the man grumbled. Chris nodded.

"Well, we might have somethin' in a couple of weeks. *Might* have somethin. I ain't makin' any promises. And you realize, if you come in here, you can't work on any of the machines. Best we might be able to do is have you sweep up, or something like that. Or … maybe bobbin boy."

When Chris heard that, he thought *"What the hell is a bobbin boy?"* It sounded like something out of "Oliver Twist," which he had read in school the month before.

The man scribbled a few things on the form and handed it back to him.

"Take that to your school now," he said. "Anybody wants to hire you, they can't do it anyways until the school gives you the real papers. Got that?"

Chris nodded again and looked at the form, then put it back in his pocket.

"If we need you, we'll call you," the man said. "It's minimum wage. Probably half days, half nights. You okay to work two to ten at night?"

He nodded again.

"All right then," the man said, hitching up his tan slacks, which had slipped well below his belly. "We'll call you if we need you."

And he waddled back into the office, leaving Chris with his signed form. Chris turned, nodded at the disinterested woman behind the glass, and walked outside. Once he got out the door, he looked at the form.

The man had put down that he would be working in a "throwing mill" and would not work more than forty hours a week during the summer, or twenty once school began. He also put down the minimum wage.

At the bottom, barely legible, was his signature. Chris wasn't sure, but he thought he could make it out.

"George Klumpfer, superintendent."

7: RECEIVING THE CALL

About a week passed, and June arrived with no word from Blake, or anyplace else. Chris had his freshly minted working papers, and was ready to go, but he began to try to figure what else he could do for the summer if he didn't get a job.

He could go swimming a lot, or maybe hang out with a few of the younger kids in the neighborhood. He could go downtown and bum around. And there was always basketball, and the television studio …

Then, one Wednesday afternoon, the phone rang. His mother almost always answered it during the day, but on this day, she was doing something in the basement. So he picked it up.

"Hello?" he said.

"Christopher Tiller?" a woman on the other end said.

His phone manner had not yet developed, so rather than say something such as "Speaking," or "This is he," he blurted out the first thing he could think of.

"Yeah!"

"Christopher, this is Marie at Blake Silk … oh, I mean … at Blake Textiles. You filled out a job application recently?"

His brain felt a rush as he heard the words.

"Oh … yeah … I mean … yes I did!"

"Well," she said, "We'd like you to come in and start work as a … let's see … well, they don't have you down for anything right now, but they'd like you to come in around one o'clock Monday afternoon. You can start on the night shift that night."

"Uh … sure!" he said.

"Just come to the office … you know, where you were when you filled out your application. And bring your working papers!"

"I will … Thank you!"

"Good bye," she said, and she hung up.

Chris ran down to the basement, where his mother was doing something with the rickety old washing machine they somehow kept running.

"Mom, Mom!" he said. "I got a job!"

His mother, having been through this all before a number of times, barely lifted her head.

"Oh, that's great hon," she said. "Remember, you gotta put whatever you make away for college!"

"Yeah, yeah," Chris said. "I start Monday night."

"Monday night?" she said, lifting her head. "You sure about that?"

"That's what they said."

"Where at?"

"Blake … Blake Silk Mill."

"Oh my," his mother said, wiping her brow. "I had a cousin who worked there years ago. But at night? How you gonna get there?"

"Well, I can walk to work," he said. "Maybe Dad can pick me up after."

"I'll have to ask him," she smiled, knowing full well that she would be the one making the decision. "But I'm sure he will. Anyway, congratulations, Chris. My baby gets his first job!"

Chris laughed; he was used to being called the "baby." He figured his brothers and sisters would still be doing it when they all had gray hair.

He turned to run back up the stairs when his mother called to him.

"Chris!" she said.

"Yeah, Mom?" he replied.

"What they gonna have you doin' there?"

He thought about what the woman said, and then about what that George fellow had said before that. He figured he didn't want to worry his mother by saying he didn't know, so he just said the first thing he remembered from his brief meeting with George.

"From what the guy said," he said with a smirk, "I'm gonna be a bobbin boy!"

8: INTO THE BREECH

Chris spent the day before his debut at Blake hearing stories about work from every relative within twenty miles of his house.

His father did everything but lay out his clothes for him. His mother seemed most concerned about whether he would eat lunch. His siblings took turns teasing him about finally getting a job, but also gave him something like three-hundred meaningless tips to help him survive his first day.

He barely slept the night before, and was up around eight in the morning. He watched a little television, went over the contents of his lunch bag with his mother, and then around noon, began to get a little queasy about what was ahead of him.

With the clock ticking toward his eventual departure for the half-hour walk to Blake, he began to panic slightly. This was not like going to a new school, where everybody was going to be his age. He was entering an adult world, and based on what he'd already encountered, the adults at Blake were somewhat lacking in the personality department.

He couldn't imagine spending eight hours a night, five nights a week, around people like the woman behind the window, or people like George. On that day, before he began his actual duties at Blake, in his mind, George Klumpfer and the woman behind the glass *were* Blake Textiles. They were all he knew of the place. He thought about them – especially about George – from the moment he hugged his mother and left his house until he finished his ascent up the hill and saw the sign on the door.

What if everybody in this building was like those two? What if he was a fairly athletic sixteen-year-old surrounded by dowdy, sour women and dumpy, grumpy men? Who could survive even a summer in a place like that?

When he entered the hallway again, he saw three other people sitting there. Two were women, probably in their twenties, and the other was a middle-aged man who appeared to be slightly mentally disabled. He sat down, saying nothing until exactly one o'clock, when the door opened and …

"Okay, everybody here?" said George, wearing the same clothes he had on when Chris first met him. He began to call out names, as if he was an Army sergeant, and wanted each person to raise his or her hand upon hearing their name.

"Adams!" One of the women raised her hand.

"Cicil … Cicilioni!" The other woman did the same.

"Murray!" No response. *"Murray!"*

George looked up and glared at Chris, who just shrugged his shoulders. George then looked at the other man, walked up to him, and said, *"Are you Murray?"*

The panicked man looked up at George as if his name had just been called to eternal damnation by the dark prince himself.

"Oh … yes … my … I'm very sorry … oh … yes … Murray … Murray!"

George shook his head and wrote something on his clipboard. Then he looked at Chris again.

"Tiller!"

Chris raised his hand half-heartedly. It was obvious he was the only one left, and he wondered why George had to go through the whole routine. He wondered what would have happened if he just sat there.

"So listen up," George barked. "My name is George Klumpfer. I'm the mill superintendent. That means I'm the boss around here. But that don't mean that you come to me with any of your problems, and it don't mean that you don't do what your immediate supervisors, your foreman and your floorlady, tell you.

"Now you are all on the two-to-ten shift … the nighttime shift … for this week. Next week, you'll do the six-to-two o'clock day shift. And that's how it's gonna go. One week days, one week nights. If you don't think you can handle that, then it's best you not start this job.

"Your foreman is going to be Tony. Your floorlady is Maggie. They run the show. The only one they answer to on the floor is me. If Tony or Maggie tell you to jump, you ask how high."

Chris must have rolled his eyes or something, because George stopped his presentation and looked at him.

"Everything okay … Tiller?" he said, looking at his clipboard.

"Oh, yeah," he said. "Fine."

George then went on some more about the minimum wage, and how anybody who stayed a year would be considered for a five-cent raise, assuming the government didn't raise the minimum again, which George seemed to think was just another step toward Communism.

Then George produced four clipboards, on which were a variety of forms. The women seemed used to them, but to Chris, they were all strange and new. The other fellow … Murray … just glared at his.

George told them to fill them out, and Chris somehow managed to figure out how to do them, although he did ask the woman named Cicilioni to help him decide what sort of tax withholding he should put down.

They were all done before Murray had really even gotten started, so the two women helped him as best they could as Chris simply looked around.

And then George came back out, gathered up their clipboards, and like the big boss he said he was, ordered his new charges into form.

"Okay, everybody up!" he said, to which they all complied. "Follow me. You're all off to the mill floor. When we get to your respective stations, you'll be dropped off and left in the charge of somebody who can show you what you'll be doing every night … well, every day and night."

Chris got in the back of the line. He wanted to be as far away from George as he could. After only two meetings with this pompous fellow, he knew that was probably a good place to be.

• • •

After a short walk through another hallway, the group reached the third floor, where the main operation took place.

George stopped before he opened the door.

"Now, by rights, you're supposed to wear ear plugs in here," he said. "I ain't got time to set you up with that now. Somebody will come around a little later tonight to set you up with that. But I gotta warn you, it's loud in there. So everybody ready?"

They thought they were ready. But when George opened the doors, it was apparent they weren't ready.

First there was the "*WHOOSH!* The women gasped. Chris felt his eyebrows arch. Murray just smiled.

Within a couple of seconds, the overwhelming sound was that of an interminable amount of machines running at tremendous speed. If you heard it from the outside, it sounded like a roar, but inside, it sounded less muffled, more concise. To Chris, it sounded as if somebody had gathered all the Lionel train engines in the world in one giant room, put them on their tracks, and threw the switch, sending their sounds cascading across the floor, and bouncing off the walls.

Chris could hear flywheels turning, and motorized arms pumping. The sounds were like one big auditory soup; it made no sense to try to identify individual elements of it. But it definitely was a sound of a specific slice of American industry. And like so many young men and women before them, the new workers realized that what went on behind the stone walls of all these so-called "silk mills" was anything but delicate.

The two women got to their work stations first. They were going to spend whatever time they remained at Blake – until lunch, a few months, perhaps the next thirty years; who knew? – working in one of the endless rows of throwing machines. They would pace from one end to another, watching for breakages, replacing empty bobbins with full ones, trying perhaps to convince themselves that they were doing something important – if not for the nation, then at least for themselves, or their ability to someday pay for Catholic school tuition for their children, or whatever incentive drove them to the mill.

Chris felt sorry for the two women; they seemed pleasant enough when they were waiting with him in the hallway. But once they were dropped off at their assigned stations, they were put in the charge of a shrewish little woman who looked to be in her mid-fifties but who, like George, really was still in her forties.

Her salt-and-pepper hair tied back so tightly as to make a librarian wince, she was wearing a patterned dress that looked as if it had been bleached so often that it might soon disintegrate if she tried to put it on. She had on black glasses, dark shoes that made her seem even more grandmotherly, and seemed to approach walking less as a means of transportation than as a method of propulsion to get her to the next person at whom she wanted to scowl.

From the instant he saw her, Chris could not conceive of this woman being physically able to smile. Her eyes, beady and dark behind the glasses, seemed to point inward, toward her nose. She wasn't cross-eyed; it was just that she seemed to constantly be honed in on something, located on the other end of that pointy nose, that required her immediate attention.

He would look into those eyes in the weeks to come, and whenever he did, he saw something at once sinister and vacant, as if they really weren't windows to a soul.

Interpersonal communication, to this woman, seemed to require only that she send out staccato, often threatening, bursts of words at human receiver after human receiver. But there was no indication that she ever really tried to figure out if those receivers were, in fact, picking up on the bursts. It was as if her mind was so filled with those bursts that she needed to emit them almost constantly; Chris got the feeling that if she ever stopped sending those bursts, or stopped darting from worker to worker, she would probably fall down dead.

Then again, he noticed that it was so loud in this place, that maybe that was the only way she knew how to talk.

As soon as the two women were put in her charge, she started harassing them as if they had been impressed into the nineteenth-century Royal Navy, and she was their merciless captain.

"You come here, you're gonna work!" she scowled at the woman named Cicilioni, who as far as Chris could tell, hadn't done a thing except smile at the shrew.

Chris felt like saying "No shit!" He didn't do that, but he did decide to clear one thing up with George.

"I guess that's Maggie?" he said.

George turned, glared for a second, and nodded his head. As the model-train sounds rattled around him, Chris began to realize that it wasn't going to be easy to hold a normal human conversation in this place.

George walked Chris and Murray through other parts of the floor before they reached an area about halfway to the other end. It was right about two o'clock, and the two newbies were taken over to the foreman's desk, which really wasn't a desk as much as it was a glorified work bench. The foreman and floorlady used it for writing, mostly, and it was loaded with various memos and other papers.

Chris noticed a short, paunchy man who definitely looked to be in his mid-forties, leaning up against the desk. He appeared to be of Italian, or some sort of southern European, descent.

Like George, he was dressed in a button-down, short-sleeved shirt, only his was a pale yellow. He had on black pants and black shoes that looked as if he probably got them from an Army-Navy surplus store.

Tony Galardi had begun working at the Blake Silk Mill just after World War II. He had been rejected for military service due to a hearing problem; Chris surmised that this was the perfect place for him, since he couldn't hear as much of the noise as everybody else.

That hearing problem also enabled Tony to be the contrast to Maggie on the floor. As foreman, he was in charge – he reported directly to George, but George didn't spend as much time on the floor as he liked people to believe, instead hanging out primarily in a small office the company had rigged up for him.

Tony was one of three foremen in the main section of the mill. He and another foreman named Ray alternated the first and second shifts every other week. Another fellow named Jake ran the overnight shift from ten in the evening until six in the morning.

Jake didn't have a floorlady – the graveyard shift crew was small, with only about a third of the machines running; besides, most of that crew had been around a long time and could handle anything on their own. But Ray had a floorlady named Molly, who had taken over for Flossie, the beloved floorlady who had worked at the plant for decades before retiring a few years earlier. Molly was no less intent on making sure things ran well than was Maggie, but her personality was quite the opposite. Whereas Maggie would cajole, threaten, and insult, Molly was more likely to prod, encourage, and help her workers get through a problem.

Ray could be a little more sarcastic than Tony, but given the minor difference between them, and the general disdain for Maggie, turnover was a lot higher on Tony's shifts.

There were some who thought Tony let Maggie push him around. He could see how it might appear that way. Basically, he preferred to let her be the pit bull, while he stayed above the fray. Tony rarely stepped in to deal with a machine operator's problems unless they specifically asked for him – something that would infuriate Maggie – or unless it was a problem requiring his physical strength, which obviously exceeded that of the little shrew.

George approached Tony, whispered something to him, and then wandered off, without so much as an introduction. He left that to the foreman.

"Hello boys," he said. "My name's Tony. I'm the foreman here. On this shift, at least. I don't know if youse guys will be on my shift permanently or not, but if it ain't me, it's Ray. We each got a floorlady you need to pay attention to. I guess you already seen Maggie?"

Chris nodded, but Murray didn't do anything, The next thing Chris knew, he and Murray were being handed time cards, and they marched over with Tony to the time clock near the entrance, where he solemnly showed them how to insert them.

"Here," he said to Chris. "You try it."

Chris had never punched a time clock before, but it took him one try to do it the right way. Murray, on the other hand, struggled with everything from putting the card in the slot right-side-up, to knowing where to put his card in the alphabetically organized rack.

After a couple of minutes, Tony got him situated, and they started to walk back toward the foreman's desk. About halfway there, a five-foot-two, one-hundred-pound obstacle stopped their progress.

"Where they going?" snarled Maggie. "They going on the lines?"

"No Maggie, they aren't," Tony responded in as soft a voice as possible given the noise. "For now we're going to have them on bobbins."

"We don't need no more bobbin boys!"

"Well that's what George told me," he said, putting his hand on Chris's shoulder. "Tiller here isn't eighteen yet, so he can't go on the lines … you know that. And …"

Tony then whispered something to Maggie; it was obvious to Chris that he was telling her that Murray was incapable of handling machine work.

"Then why do they bring these people in here?" Maggie grumbled as she walked away, barely acknowledging any of them.

Tony sighed and waved the two of them toward the bobbin station, which was adjacent to the foreman's desk. Chris noticed that the bobbins on this station were metallic, and looked like spools of thread somebody had blown up to about four times their normal size. They were placed on metal racks, and they came to the bobbin station after they'd been used up on various machines in the plant. They usually had oil, or pieces of thread, or some unwanted cardboard on them.

These bobbin boys had a simple task – take the dirty bobbins off the wooden pallet on which they'd been dropped off, clean them, and put them back on another pallet to be sent off to be re-filled. It was a mundane, grubby, monotonous task. And in this part of the plant, with machines humming and roaring on both sides, it was like doing the job inside of a ringing bell. The ear plugs George had promised wouldn't be handed out for a week, and by that point, Chris had learned that nobody wore them anyway. To do so branded one a pussy – it was preferable to risk hearing loss than to risk that label.

Tony took Chris and Murray over to a man named Frank, another older-looking man in his forties. Hair slicked back, with heavy glasses, a gut hanging over a grimy green T-shirt, and wearing a pair of work pants that Chris figured got rinsed out about once a week, Frank was nominally the head of the bobbin boys in this area. As far as Chris could tell, Frank was fairly dim-witted, and his main qualification for leadership was that he was older than anybody else in his section.

Chris and Murray were going to join two other guys. One was an oafish character in his late twenties who also seemed a bit slow. The other was a little hippie type, probably in his late teens or early twenties.

Murray paired up with the oaf, later identified as Lawrence. About ten minutes into their pairing, they started arguing, as Murray did not perform up to Lawrence's specifications. Tony had to come over to quiet them down – even among the noise of the machines, their cackling was audible.

A few minutes later, after Tony had made a phone call, a woman from the office came up and Murray was gone. Chris never heard another word about him.

Before all this happened, though, Chris got paired up with Jeff Ryan, the little hippie guy. Jeff was only about five-foot-three – he might have been a centimeter or two taller than Maggie – and he had black hair that fell well to his shoulder blades. He wore a headband that looked as if it came right off the front counter of one of the head shops in town. He wore jeans and tan boots, and was wearing a black T-shirt, although he had a long-sleeved Army shirt he wore when he wasn't up to his elbows in bobbins.

He didn't have much competition, but Jeff certainly was the winner among this motley contingent when it came to both smarts and personality. Over the next few days, Chris would see him figure out something that Frank couldn't comprehend. Frank was pretty miserable and Lawrence was obnoxious, but Jeff had a buoyant personality, especially within the walls of Blake, where he was unable to access the copious amounts of marijuana he inhaled when he wasn't at work.

When Chris and Murray were sent over to the station, Jeff made a beeline for Chris, who except for being a bit younger, about a half-a-foot taller, and having shorter hair (his only made it about to his shoulders), seemed more like him than Murray.

"Hey man, welcome to the Blake!" he said, referring to the mill the way most of the workers did, with the definitive article in front of the name. "My name's Jeff!"

"Hey, Jeff," said Chris. "I'm Chris."

"Well, man, let's get you started then," Jeff said. "First thing you gotta do is get yourself a rag. C'mon, I'll show you where the stuff is."

They went over to a drawer, from which Jeff pulled out a white rag that had obviously been through numerous wash cycles, along with a sheet of sandpaper and a roll of masking tape.

"Here's your rag," he said, handing it to Chris. "You mainly use that to wipe the oil off these bobbins. They come back with oil on 'em lots of times, and you gotta wipe the oil off or Frank'll start bitchin' and … well, it's a pain in the ass. Just wipe the oil off."

Jeff then took what looked like a stick out of his back pocket.

"Now, the other thing you gotta do is make one of these," he said, holding it in the air. "Looks like a stick, don't it? Well, it ain't. What you do is, you take this sandpaper like this …"

He started folding the sandpaper around itself, about a half-an-inch wide. By pulling it tighter with each turn, he managed to make a device that was as hard as a wooden stick.

"Then you get the tape and you tape it up real good in the center, see?" he said as he did that. "That keeps it together. You got a little sanding stick here, and you use that to get the excess yarn off the bobbins."

The metal bobbins were about the size of an oil can. There were eight on each rack, and the racks were stacked on the pallets about six to eight high. Frank made a few trips each shift to collect dirty ones, but the cleaned bobbins were picked up by another worker who took them away to be refilled.

Tony also gave Frank a few other duties each shift – sweeping stairwells, cleaning ashtrays, gathering up used cardboard – that kept him occupied, and pretty much out of the hair of the bobbin boys who were actually doing the work. For the most part, on this shift, that had been Jeff. Lawrence was the slowest worker of them all – George once told Tony that he was the slowest bobbin boy he'd ever seen – and they'd had a hard time keeping even one other bobbin boy for more than a few days on this shift.

Ray and Molly's shift had a full crew, but working with the likes of Maggie, Frank, and Lawrence made this shift tough to keep staffed.

About ten minutes after getting his rag and making his sanding stick, Chris had blown past Lawrence and Frank, and was not far off the pace set by Jeff.

"How long you been here?" Chris asked Jeff as he tried to keep up with him.

"About a year," Jeff said. "It ain't too bad. It's a job."

"Where you from?" said Chris. "I live about a half-hour's walk from here."

"You walk? Oh man, not me! I live over on the South Side. My brother gives me a ride up and back. He has a Dodge I wanna buy from him for a hundred bucks once I save up enough money."

After about an hour, Chris started thinking how he'd made enough money to get a slice of pizza and a Coke downtown on Saturday. He was trying not to think about things like that, but this job was so mundane, so mind-numbing, that any thoughts were welcome. He later learned to start tying each hour into progress toward a particular album he wanted – "Okay, seven o'clock, that's halfway to The Who's new album!"

But on this first day, with time dragging, the thoughts were of pizza. After he'd wiped and scratched and stacked who-knows-how-many bobbins, he felt Jeff tap him on the arm.

"C'mon man, four o'clock!"

Chris wasn't sure of the significance, but he noticed that Jeff had put down the tools of the trade.

"C'mon man, four o'clock!" Jeff said. "You know … it's time."

"Time for what?"

"Break time, man! Time for a break!"

Jeff pulled a pack of Marlboros from his pocket. Chris smoked only now and then, but he got the symbolism – it was time to go smoke or stand around and watch others smoke somewhere.

But where?

"Don't know where to go?" Jeff asked. "Follow me."

"Where we goin'?" Chris said.

Jeff threw his head back as if he'd just been asked the most preposterous question on the planet.

"Where else?" he said. "To the john!"

9: THE SMOKE-FILLED CHAMBER

If George's opening the doors to the mill floor had been an assault on Chris Tiller's auditory senses, then Jeff Ryan doubled down with an attack on the new guy's visual and olfactory senses when he opened the door to the men's room.

As soon as the door opened, Chris noticed a virtual cloud of cigarette smoke heading his way. Four men were in the room smoking, and with just a one-foot-by-two-feet window on the opposite end to the door providing ventilation, the air was practically painted with the fumes of human-exhaled tar and nicotine, among other elements.

To the left of the door was a metal divider, on the other side of which were three tightly compressed and old-style urinals – the ones that reached all the way to the floor.

Beyond the divider in the direction away from the door were two toilet stalls on the left, and two sinks attached to the wall on the right. A radiator bulged from underneath the window, which was reinforced with thick glass and chicken wire. The window was propped open, but being that it was summer, the air outside was relatively stale, and not much in the way of fresh air was even attempting to fight its way through the toxic haze.

Two young men were leaning with their backs to the window, and two more were propped up against the sinks. Jeff immediately plopped down on the floor close to the door and lit up a Marlboro – just about everybody at the Blake smoked Marlboros or Winstons. Chris wasn't sure where to go, so he sort of nudged himself in between Jeff and another fellow.

The other thing Chris noticed about this room was that the sound of the machinery died down. The doors were made of heavy, American-made steel, and as much as they trapped the smoke and the other smells of the men's room in, they kept the noise of the plant out.

The two young men leaning against the window were Brian and Russell, both about nineteen years old. Brian had shorter hair than Russell, whose hair was about as long as Jeff's. He also wore a headband, although it was just a plain green one and not as elaborate as the one Jeff had.

They were dressed in jeans and T-shirts, but what set them apart from Jeff and Chris were their aprons. Being over eighteen, they were able to work on the machines, and aprons were part of the standard garment for those who did such work.

"Hey, you hippies," said Jeff after he'd sat down. "This here's Chris. This is his first night. Hey man, it's his first break!"

"Who let these bobbin boys in here?" joked Russell, who reached down and gave Jeff a seventies-style locked-thumbs handshake. "New guy, eh? New guy for Maggie to fuck with!"

Everybody but Jeff and Chris laughed.

"Naw, she won't mess with him yet," Jeff said. "He ain't on a machine." He turned and looked up at Chris. "You ain't eighteen yet, are you?"

Chris shook his head.

"So he'll just work with us and she won't bother him. She'll screw with Frank."

"Yeah, Frank!" giggled Brian.

They all laughed, and Russell made a goofy-face, implying that Frank was a moron.

"Frank … the guy we're working with?" Chris said.

"Yeah, the old guy with all the greasy shit in his hair," Jeff said. "Forty-five years old ... and he's still a bobbin boy!"

"Yeah," said Russell. "But he's the *leader* of the bobbin boys!"

All but Chris paused to smoke. The other two guys who were in the room left, leaving just the four of them there.

"Did anybody see if Frank has a bottle in his apron tonight?" said Brian.

"Naw ... he only does that when he's on days!" said Jeff. "That's when he gets the balls to think he can argue with Maggie!"

"Yeah ... balls out of a bottle!" Russell said.

Jeff rose and with his free hand, pretended to take a toke from a joint.

"Now me," he said, "I need to do this..."

He took a massive breath as if he was taking a similarly sized toke; it was so hard, Chris thought it might make Jeff pass out.

"...That's when I be ready to give Maggie some shit!"

Everybody laughed. Russell looked at his watch, tapped Brian on the arm, and they both crushed out their cigarettes.

"Yeah, and you ain't never done it, have you?" he said. "Anyways, it's time to go back!"

"You mean before Maggie comes in here and gets us?" said Brian.

"Oh man, don't make me puke!" said Russell. "I got a better idea ... send in that blonde on number twenty-three!"

Russell grabbed his crotch as if he was getting oral sex; Brian laughed and left, but Russell waited a moment. Chris, meanwhile, was trying to keep up with the inside humor, and without thinking, sat down on one of the sinks bolted into the wall. Jeff noticed it, but didn't say anything as he got up.

"Hey Russell, anybody seen Claude tonight?" he said.

"I think he called in sick," Russell said.

Jeff laughed and shook his head. "Yeah, he's sick! He's so sick he'll have to go to the Buccaneer for treatment tonight!"

Jeff and Russell laughed, but Chris was taken aback.

"The Buccaneer? That crazy bar where they always have fights and they're always getting stabbed? I only live two blocks from there!"

Jeff and Russell both stared at him. Everybody in town knew that the Buccaneer was located in the black part of town.

"Where the hell you live?" Jeff said, looking amazed. "On Hamilton Street or something?"

"No way!" said Chris. "I live on Dickson Street, and we never go up there. And they never come down our way. But it is only two blocks away … We hear the sirens every night around midnight. … But who … who's this Clyde, anyway?"

"Claude!" yelled Jeff. "He's one of your co-workers, man!"

"Yeah," laughed Russell. "Especially if you's … *'woy-kin nights!'* "

Jeff gave Russell a high-five and they both laughed. Chris still didn't know what they were talking about until Jeff tapped him on the chest.

"Listen man," he said. "Claude is a black guy who works here on our shift. I guess he was in Vietnam before he came here. He's technically a bobbin boy too, but he never cleans no bobbins. Mostly he does whatever needs to get done around here. He does all the heavy stuff, ya know? He fixes shit when it breaks, he hauls out stuff when it piles up. I've seen him climb up on top of machines and get the line moving when it stops."

"Yeah," said Russell, apparently imitating Claude again. "He does *'everybody's job!'* "

"Really?" said Chris.

"Well, that's what he says, anyway …" said Jeff.

At that moment, the men's room door opened, and George entered. George never took a leak or a dump in this men's room, but he occasionally came in to wash his hands if he just finished doing something dirty. Most of the workers knew that was just an excuse to spy on them, but the mill had no union, so they couldn't stop him from coming in.

George's face usually was the color of oatmeal that sat around all morning, but when he was pissed off, he could turn almost scarlet. That color change took place in about three seconds after he got his first look at Chris sitting on the sink.

"What the fuck are you doing?" he roared. "Get the fuck off that sink!"

Jeff and Russell backed toward the window. Chris wasn't sure what the problem was.

"If I ever … I mean … if I *ever* … see you sitting there again like that, I'll run your ass out of here! Understand?"

With George six inches from his face, with George's breath making him wish he could inhale some more second-hand smoke, Chris took just a second to realize that he had to get his butt in motion – literally! He dropped it off the sink and stood up straight as George remained in his face.

"Who the hell you think you are?" George said, not screaming, but in a slow burn that made Chris wish he still was screaming. "You could pull that God-damned sink right out of the wall sitting on it like that! Who the hell you think you are?"

His vocal chords locked, Chris could only stare at the mill honcho. George, meanwhile, decided he wasn't in the mood for an audience.

"Ain't break time over?" he said, glaring at Russell, in particular. Their second cigarettes of the break not quite down to the butt end, Jeff and Russell immediately tossed them to the floor and started for the door. They squeezed past George and out to the rumbling machinery.

George glared at Chris again, pointed at him and walked out.

Chris wondered how anybody worked at this place! Moronic co-workers, bosses who fancied themselves as dictators. He was still shaking slightly, alone in the men's room he'd only entered for the first time a few minutes before, when he heard the door opening again.

He was sure George had returned, in fact, to run his ass out of the joint.

Instead, blasting past the world of gray and green T-shirts and skinny hippie wannabes, and into the startled, shaken world of the sixteen-year-old first-timer walked a creature of black and orange and gold, obliterating and overtaking all that had gone before him in the little one-window refuge of the denizens of the Blake.

10: LORD OF THE BREAK ROOM

"Oh, man … Oh, lordy, lordy!" he bellowed. "Where, oh where are all my fellow workers?"

He was about five-foot-eleven, with the build of a welterweight, or maybe even a light-heavyweight, fighter. His upper body tapered from broad, ripped shoulders, down past a bulging chest to a tight, smaller abdomen. His biceps were slightly out of proportion – on the large side – even to that torso. His forearms appeared powerful, as did his hands.

He was not quite as dark as some African or West Indian people Chris had met, most of them missionaries at his church. But he was darker than most of the black people Chris knew from school.

He was in his mid-twenties, and his hair was short – he did not have anything close to the Afro style popular at the time. He had large, powerful facial features. His eyes, nose and mouth all exerted power – and that was before he opened the latter. And his wardrobe! Even if he had been scrawny, his wardrobe would have made him stand out. He was wearing a short-sleeved yellow shirt, but it was nothing like the one George or Tony had on. This was, in the parlance of the time, a "body shirt." It was stretched out to accentuate every aspect of his torso, with no space at all anywhere between fabric and skin. And rather than being of the button-down variety, it was one he pulled over his head, with just a small zipper on the front neck.

His pants were yellow and orange, with alternating vertical stripes of each color. They were closely pressed to his body, from the waist down. He had on a white belt, but jet black shoes – boots, really.

As he entered, he was taking out a cigarette as if he was Robert Mitchum entering a bar in some old black-and-white *film noir.* He had big teeth, and one of them was made of gold. Chris had never seen that before, either.

What could this sixteen-year-old white kid say when this sort of man walked into the room? If George intimidated Chris based on his position and his status, this man intimidated Chris … by being *this man*!

He walked by Chris, staring at him, then took a seat on the radiator. He didn't hesitate to hop up on top of it, as if the very idea of somebody in this building coming in to challenge him about it was inconceivable.

"Hey, man," he said to Chris. "I ain't never seen you before! You new here?"

Chris gulped. "Uh-huh!" he said.

"You a bobbin boy, then, huh?"

Chris nodded.

"Well man, that's what they say I am, too," he laughed. "But what I *do* is … I *do everybody's* job, you see? I mean … well, I do my own job first … *then* I do everybody else's job!"

Chris had heard he might say that. But there was something about hearing it from him!

"But you'll find out," the man said.

Chris couldn't say anything because he was still shaken from the encounter with George.

"Hey man," the man said. "What the fuck is the matter with you, man?"

Chris gulped and started to speak.

"Well … uh … uh … they said you weren't working tonight."

"Me? I ain't working? Who said that? Oh … you mean those dudes? Man, you ought not to listen to them dudes! They don't know which end of their ass to back out the door first. Where'd they say I was?"

Chris began to form a word, but was cut off.

"Oh shit … lemme guess … the Buccaneer?"

Chris nodded.

"Man, it ain't like I *live* in that shit hole! Fuck, man, I go up there once in a while. But what the fuck I tellin' you for? You ain't old enough to go take a piss in that place!"

"I know, but I only live a couple blocks from there."

"No shit! I bet your momma told you to stay away from us folks up there, eh?"

Chris didn't respond. He smiled and started to walk away.

"Hey man, what's your name anyway?"

"Chris."

"Chris? Shit, that ain't too far from my name … Claude," he said, taking a long drag on his cigarette. "I bet you real surprised, meetin' that big, bad Claude dude you been hearin' about, right man?"

Chris nodded.

"Hey, Chris, man!" Claude said. "You all right, man. I like a dude who don't come in here shootin' his mouth off … that's my job! Got it? *My job* … like everything else around here?"

They both laughed.

"But hey, man, you better get back out there fast, before Frank and Maggie and George and all them mother fuckers come lookin' for you."

"George already did," Chris said.

"He did?" said Claude. "Well fuck him! He's all mouth, man! All fuckin' mouth, man! He sure don't fuck with me!"

Claude took another long drag. Chris couldn't remember ever seeing a man so secure, so sure that in a world filled with Georges and Maggies, nobody was going to come into this men's room and give him a world of shit.

"So get the fuck outta here," he said with a smile. "And hey, man, remember one thing … don't you come lookin' for me to do your work too … ya hear?"

Chris looked back and tried to smile, but nothing he could muster could even approach the big smile radiating from above the radiator.

So he sighed and reached for the door. His first break was over. He wondered if he could stay sane until another one.

11: TALES FROM THE NIGHT SHIFT

Chris spent another hour-and-a-half wiping and scraping until lunch. He went outside for a half-hour and ate his sandwich in solitude near the plant entrance, trying to maintain the mindset that he was working toward slices of pizza, record albums, and maybe even a copy of Playboy – if he could get somebody to buy it for him.

Then he went back to work, and it was starting to feel as if this night would never end. Would every night be like this? How could he possibly make it through five of these in a row? And then come back for five more? And five more?

A few minutes before eight o'clock, as darkness was just starting to creep down upon the town outside, Jeff tapped him on the arm again, and signaled that they should return to the men's room for the final break of the night.

The eight o'clock session in the men's room was quite unlike the one at four. For one thing, George had gone home. He could, of course, pop back in unannounced and just happen to walk into the men's room, but that almost never happened.

Then there was the fact that almost all the shifts in the mill were staggered, and that many of the workers who had been there at four were either gone, or were about to leave. The two workers who had been in the men's room when he got there at four, for example, were leaving at eight, so they were going to be out the door and on their way home.

The biggest difference, though, was just in the attitude of those taking their breaks. At four, many of them had only been in the building for about two hours, and had a long shift ahead of them. The break represented a chance to analyze what was to come.

At eight, though, it was just a matter of making it for a little while longer, and then they could go home. The late break seemed to be both retrospective and anticipatory. The sun that was beaming through the little window at four o'clock had pretty much set; the light was now artificial, making those in the room seem somehow larger than they might have during the day.

Some of the workers used the last break to look back on the events of the shift, but others talked about what they would do after work.

When Chris and Jeff walked into the men's room at eight, Brian and Russell were there, looking more tired than they had at four. Claude was seated on the radiator again.

They were joined by a strange fellow, one Chris had never seen before. He was a frail, almost dainty-looking man, probably in his twenties, with a mop of red hair. He was standing awkwardly next to Claude, looking almost off-balance. To Chris, he almost appeared crippled.

He was holding his cigarette gingerly, and when he inhaled, he drew long, exaggerated breaths. When he exhaled, he seemed almost afraid, as if he might not catch his breath on the return.

Claude was talking when Jeff and Chris walked in, although Brian and Russell appeared to be mumbling between themselves.

"Now ya'll just wait a minute," Claude said, emphasizing the point with his right hand, which was holding his cigarette. (Claude, unlike almost everybody else in the room, smoked Kools.)

"I ain't gonna sit here and listen to ya'll bitch about Maggie til closin' time," he said. "You don't see her pushin' me around, do ya?"

"She knows better," said Russell.

Claude hopped down from the radiator. He seemed almost evangelical.

"Now, y'all listen to me," he said, practically singing out the next few words. "All … you … guys … workin' … nights … Listen to me, now! I come in here every day … and I know I got a job to do. And I do my job …"

Jeff, Brian and Russell all laughed. They'd heard all this before, but they never got tired of it.

"And when I'm done doin' my job …" he said, beginning to point at various others in the room, "then I do Jeff's job … and then I do Brian's job … and then I do Russell's job!"

They were all laughing as he popped back up on the radiator, and began actually singing the previous line, almost as if he was performing a do-wop song.

"I know I got a job … know I got a job … to dooooo!!!"

Even Chris was laughing now. The guy could really sing!

"Yeah, Claude, old Maggie ain't gonna fuck with you!" Russell said.

Claude bounced back off the radiator. He pointed at Russell again with the hand with the Kool in it, and made a nasty face, as if he'd just eaten something sour.

"Oooh … man … don't even use them words in the same sentence, man!" he said. "Shit … Maggie … fuck? Oh man!"

They all laughed. Claude just as quickly pivoted verbally and changed the subject … somewhat.

"Man, I'm gonna get me over to the Buccaneer tonight," he said, and then he pointed directly at Chris. "And I don't wanna see none of *you* over there!"

"You gonna get you some woman tonight, Claude?" Russell said.

"No, man, some woman's gonna get *me!*"

Brian got up and left. Chris got the impression that Brian didn't care much for Claude's sexual bragging, but his pal Russell seemed to love it.

"We gonna read about you in the newspaper tomorrow, Claude?" he said.

Claude was pacing now, and most of his looks went not to Russell, who was asking the questions, nor to Jeff, but to Chris.

"Shit, you mean getting' shot or stabbed or something? Naw … not me man! I just gotta be careful I don't end up like Jose did."?

"Jose?" Jeff asked. "You mean that fighter?"

"Yeah, shit, man, you know what happened to him!"

Claude looked around. He realized that Jeff and Russell were familiar with the story, and that Richie – the guy with the red hair – had heard it many times. But Chris was clueless. So here was a chance to tell the story again!

Claude popped back up on the radiator and, like children waiting to hear a familiar old tale from their grandpa, the others listened.

"Man, that Jose, man, he was a damned good fighter. Shit … he fought in those fights every month over at the arena downtown, and he really beat the shit outta those mother fuckers. He was gonna go fight in Madison Square Garden, man … in fuckin' *New York!* Mother fucker was gonna fight some big contender or somethin'. Mighta gotten a title fight outta that … or that's what they said, anyways."

Claude took a long drag of his Kool. Richie took such a long drag of his Winston that Chris wondered if he was going to breathe again.

"Then you know what happened to the mother fucker!"

The other three nodded as Chris looked at Claude, whom he realized was probably telling the story for his benefit.

"Goes out with some bitch he met at the Buccaneer, and he's drivin' on that road … what the fuck's it called … Meadow Ridge Road or somethin' like that?"

"Yeah," Russell said. "Right where there's a T in the road where the high school is …"

"Right … so the mother fucker is drivin'," Claude continued, steering an imaginary wheel in front of him, "and he's goin' about a hundred miles an hour, and this bitch is givin' him head like she's a fuckin' Electrolux, man!"

Chris felt himself gasp as the others laughed.

"Yeah … she's suckin' him off so fuckin' hard I'm surprised she didn't inhale his dick … but anyway … well, any of you ever seen that pole up there, man?"

That was when Chris, who was headed for his senior year at that high school, thought about the solid steel pole near the front entrance. The pole was dented at about a twenty-degree angle.

"Man, that fuckin' pole was made outta solid steel … and those two mother fuckers hit it at a hundred miles per hour, with her mouth on Jose's cock and suckin' away … and that pole, man … it looks like a fuckin' 'C' right about now."

Despite their familiarity with the tale, everybody stopped laughing.

"They had to pry them two outta that car," Claude said, sucking on his Kool. "Shit, from what I heard, they couldn't tell where she ended and Jose started!"

Chris Tiller was sixteen years old, and no choirboy. But he'd never heard anything like this!

"Man, there ain't nothin' wrong with gettin' sucked off!" Claude said. "But I ain't drivin' into no steel pole for no bitch, I don't care how good she sucks cock!"

Russell started to smile.

"Whatcha thinkin' about boy?" Claude said.

"Aw … I just wish Maggie would go like that!"

Claude laughed and threw his cigarette butt on the floor.

"Maggie ain't even sucked on a *lollipop* in her whole life!" he said.

"Well, how about George?" Russell said.

"You want George to be givin' or gettin'?" said Claude.

"Don't matter," said Russell. "Long as he hits the pole!"

Claude smiled and hopped off the radiator. As he passed by Chris, he playfully made a fist, which made Chris wince. Claude smiled, his gold tooth the first thing Chris saw.

"Y'all better watch what you say about the bosses in here," he said, leaning up against one of the toilet stalls. "I remember a couple of years ago, I had to come in here just to take a piss … wasn't gonna smoke or nothin' … just to take a leak. But this guy I knew was in here and he had the red ass about somethin', man. So I lit up a smoke and next thing I knew, he was bitchin' up a storm about George. He was mother fuckin' George all over the place. He was tellin' me George was a cocksucker and a mother fucker and George better hope he never saw him outside of work, because he'd kick the shit out of him."

Claude stopped and looked up at the ceiling for a moment.

"Man, I musta had an angel or somethin' with me that day, because for once in my life, man, I didn't say a word. Y'all know that ain't easy for me!"

They all laughed.

"Anyway, I'm stayin' quiet, ya know, and then I don't know what, but for some reason, I looked down. And I saw some feet in one of the stalls! And I'm thinkin', 'Holy shit, them ain't no workin' man's shoes!' I knew they had to belong to a boss. Then it hit me. 'Holy shit! That's mother-fuckin' George in there!' "

Chris smiled, recalling his encounter with George earlier in the day.

"So I kept quiet, but I was tryin' to motion to this fucker to shut the fuck up … you know, to be quiet," Claude said, putting his index finger to his lips. "But the mother fucker kept talkin' for another minute about how he was gonna give George all this shit!"

Claude stopped and started to nod his head and smile.

"Well then, sure as shit, the stall door swings open, and out comes George … his face was as frozen as the fuckin' North Pole. He don't say a word. He just comes out, washes his hands, and goes out the door."

"What did the other guy do?" said Jeff.

"Oh man, he looked like he just got his balls caught in the conveyor belt. He sat down on the floor, and he said, 'Holy shit, I'm fucked!' What was I supposed to say? I said, 'Yes you are, man. You are fucked!' He went back out there, and I thought the mother fucker was gonna cry!"

At that, Chris heard Richie speak for the first time. Richie had a fairly pronounced lisp, a pretty serious speech impediment in which he seemed to spit many of his words.

"Yeah," he said. "That guy didn't last much longer!"

Claude looked at Richie, but didn't say anything.

"He worked a couple more days and left," he said. "I swear, I never saw that cat come in here again … even to take a piss! He must have held it every night until he could go out into the woods at lunch time!"

He raised a finger in the air, as if he was about to deliver the moral of the story.

"And it just goes to show you guys … Before you talk any shit about the boss, you gotta make sure the boss ain't *takin'* a shit!"

Richie gave Claude a high-five, and then he, Jeff, and Russell went back out onto the floor. Claude looked at Chris again, but didn't say anything. He just began singing his refrain again:

When I come in here every day, I know I got a job, know I got a job, to do. And when I do that job, I do Dave's job, and Steve's job, and …

Claude walked toward the door, put his hand on the door and, still singing, looked back and Chris and smiled as he sang.

Chris didn't know who Dave and Steve were. He just wondered how they got into the song, and how long it would be before he got there … if he *ever* got there.

12: BREVETED TO BIG BOBBINS

For the rest of his first week at the Blake, Chris did his job, went on his breaks, joked around with Claude and the other guys, saw Maggie glaring at him, and basically just tried to get used to life as a mill worker.

His internal count had him figuring that after he gave his mother most of his check, he'd have enough to get at least two albums, as much pizza and soda as he wanted, and any other small items he might desire. He decided to hold off on the Playboy until later in the summer, though.

By Friday night, he was cleaning bobbins more quickly than anybody, including Jeff. On one or two occasions, Tony even went to him first on a bobbin-related issue. He could sense that Frank was getting frustrated, and even Jeff limited his conversations with him.

When he came back from his eight o'clock break on Friday night – a break that saw him alone in the men's room for almost its entirety, as Claude was doing something on the loading dock, Richie and Russell had called in sick, and Jeff decided not to join him – Tony intercepted him on his way back to the bobbin area.

"Tiller," he said. "See you a minute?"

"Sure," Chris said, walking over to the foreman's area. Tony motioned for him to come close to him, so that Frank and the rest couldn't hear.

"Now, you know that on Monday, you come in at six in the morning, right?"

"Yeah," he said. "Looking forward to it."

"Well, whatever," Tony said. "But I want you to know we're gonna shuffle things around a little bit starting Monday. When you come in, don't come over to this bobbin area. You're gonna be moving to big bobbins starting Monday."

Chris gasped. Big bobbins? Really?

About a third of the machines on the throwing floor used the smaller, metallic, oil-can-shaped bobbins on which Frank, Jeff, Lawrence, and Chris had been working all week. The majority used a different type; a wooden bobbin, shaped like a large candle, about a foot high, on a small, round wooden base. Cleaning them required a different approach than did working on the smaller ones.

For starters, you couldn't just sand things off the wooden bobbins. Sandpaper would scratch their finish, and if somebody like Lawrence, who had the deft touch of an ogre, ever tried to clean them with a sanding stick, the company would end up throwing out half its expensive supply. Most of the cleaning of the wooden bobbins involved much more intense removal of the oil and other byproducts that accumulated on them.

The other difference was even more crucial. Stacking the smaller bobbins was a relatively menial task; it really could be done by anybody. The wooden bobbins, being much taller, were therefore more difficult to stack. A stack of five racks of the metal bobbins might reach about three feet high. A stack of five racks of wooden bobbins would reach at least twice as high. Maneuvering them in the tight environment of the mill floor was not easy, and a tipped load could cause serious problems if thirty or so wooden bobbins crashed into sensitive machinery.

Yet here was Chris Tiller, one week into his first-ever job, sixteen years old, being put in charge of what essentially was his own department.

The big bobbin boy was on his own. There was one on each shift, and he was responsible for everything it took three or four of them to do on the smaller bobbins, with much more margin for error.

And oh, Maggie probably spent about seventy-five percent of her time working with the machines that used big bobbins. She was notorious for being a thorn in the side of her shift's big bobbin boy.

But what could he do? It was a promotion … kind of! His mother and father would be happy. And if he could get some overtime out of it, his father would be ecstatic!

• • •

When Chris got into his father's car at the end of his shift Friday night, he was tired, but somewhat excited to have a free weekend ahead of him. There was something about working all week that made a weekend a lot more fun than the previous one had been.

Tom Tiller wasn't exactly crazy about having to go out every night to pick his son up outside the Blake, but he had been there every night so far. He had his own factory job, which began at seven in the morning. When he was in his twenties, he could stay up until past midnight drinking at some corner bar, and then be one of the first ones on the line at seven. He could do this five nights a week.

But he gave up that lifestyle when his family came on the scene, and in recent years, he was often out cold by the time the late news came on.

However, when Chris got his first job, Tom was pressed into service, as he had been with all his other children, as an on-call driver. For this summer, he fully expected to alternate driving to the Blake according to his son's schedule. When Chris was working nights, Chris would walk to work and Tom would pick him up after ten.

The following week, when Chris went on days, Tom would get up even earlier than usual to run him to work for his scheduled start at six in the morning. Then Chris would walk home.

Tom had been through a tougher schedule than this. One of his daughters had been a waitress for a while at an all-night diner; she usually got off work at two in the morning. Now *that* cut into just about all of his non-working activities!

When Chris left the mill on Friday night, Tom was in the parking lot. The Blake parking lot could hold scores of cars, and around four in the afternoon, it could get pretty crowded. By nighttime, though, it was usually about half-empty, with only the graveyard-shift workers there by about eleven or so.

"Hey Dad," Chris said as he got in the car. "Guess what?"

"Huh," Tom said, not expecting anything important.

"I guess I got some kind of promotion tonight."

"*What?*" Tom said, holding off on turning the key in the ignition once he heard this news. "What kind of a promotion do you get after a week of a summer job?"

"Well, it ain't more money or anything," Chris said. "But they're putting me on big bobbins starting Monday."

"Big bobbins?"

"Yeah … I'm not sure what that means myself … but they said it means I'll be working by myself instead of with those other guys."

"Wow," Tom said as he started the car. "Any chance of overtime?"

Chris knew that was coming. His father was from a generation that grew up during the Great Depression, a generation that considered overtime practically a gift from the gods, never to be rejected, scoffed at, or even taken lightly.

"No, Dad, no overtime!" Chris said. "Can you let me get used to working forty hours first?"

"Well, don't ever refuse any overtime, you know!"

"Okay, okay!" Chris said impatiently. He didn't say much the rest of the way home.

After hanging out with his friends and going to the movies Saturday, Chris went to church on Sunday morning. He tried to watch a baseball game on television, but he started to find it difficult to concentrate on the game, or anything else, for that matter.

By about four in the afternoon, he was feeling even more distracted. By six, his mind felt as if it was being squeezed in his head.

What was this? He'd felt strange on Sunday afternoons and evenings prior to going back to school on some Mondays – particularly if there was a test coming up. He usually felt something like this the day before football practice started every year – but that was more a sense of "let's get this over with for two weeks."

This feeling was unique … and very strange! Was it starting the day shift? Was it the new "big bobbin" gig? Did he worry about having lunch at ten in the morning?

He even went for a long walk right before dark, hoping to tire himself out so he could get some sleep. But it didn't work. By eleven, his parents were fast asleep in preparation for their own early start in the morning. Everybody else in the house was either asleep or content.

But the new prince of the big bobbins was a nervous wreck! This was only supposed to be a summer job … and it had only been a week! He'd never heard of Claude and Maggie and Tony until a couple of days ago … now they dominated his every thought!

This went on all night. He was flirting with an ulcer … unless somebody could put this summer-job-at-the- mill thing in perspective!

13: THE DAYS OF HIS LIFE

The strains of a Three Dog Night song crept out of Tom Tiller's AM car radio as he chugged along the nearly deserted streets of town about twenty minutes to six the following morning.

Next to him, a sleep-deprived, but still adrenaline-rushed, sixteen-year-old sat with a small lunch bag, wearing a light blue T-shirt, jeans, and a new pair of work boots his mother had picked up over the weekend at a local discount store.

It was dark when they left the house, but in the ten minutes or so that it took them to drive to the mill, the sun had started to peek out over the summer darkness. This was the first of many new experiences for Chris; he had just gotten used to arriving at work in the heat and light of the day, and going into the darker environment of the mill then. Now he was entering the mill while it was still relatively dark outside; there was no sensory transition once he got inside.

There was also the issue of the six o'clock start time. He'd been going to school for a dozen years, so it wasn't as if he wasn't used to starting his day in the morning. *But six o'clock?* Who started that early? Even his Dad didn't start work until seven!

Before Jeff had nudged him to take his first four o'clock break on the night shift, he hadn't thought much about breaks or lunch hours. And over a few days, he'd settled into something of a routine on the night shift.

He wondered what in the world this schedule would be like. His first break was going to be at eight in the morning; who was going to be in the men's room at eight in the morning? Quite a few of the machine operators just came in around then. He couldn't imagine having Claude recite his "boxer and a blowjob" tale at that hour!

Then there was lunch. Ten in the morning? That's what they said! His mother gave him a sandwich, but really … shouldn't she have just thrown in a waffle or something?

And he didn't even want to think about his final break, at noon. He couldn't see much benediction going on then!

When his father pulled up to the mill, he wished Chris good luck.

"Now you're gonna walk home, right?" he said.

Chris nodded and got out of the car. Father-son dialogue in the early seventies rarely extended beyond such non-verbal communication.

Tom drove away, and Chris entered the mill. The first thing he noticed when he got to the floor was the difference in the sound.

When he'd entered at two in the afternoon, the floor was pretty much running at full capacity. Except for a few machines down for maintenance, every line was going full tilt, and the army of Lionel locomotives seemingly numbered in the millions.

But at six, only the machines that had been running overnight could be heard. The sound went from a locomotive army to something one might hear at a holiday model railroading show. It was a slight hum, and for the first time, the sound of Chris punching the time clock could be heard in spite of the sound of the mill's machinery.

Chris later learned that it wasn't until after eight when the Lionels really started roaring.

After he punched in, he really didn't know where to go. He figured he should seek out Tony, but Tony wasn't around. Maggie was, leaning over the foreman's desk writing something. He didn't want anything to do with Maggie at six in the morning! He couldn't imagine any man, woman, or beast who would! So he ducked into the men's room.

There were two fellows in there. One was an older fellow whose name he never did learn, and who never said a word to him all summer.

The other guy was a character to whom he took an immediate liking. He later found out his name was Will, but it would be some time before either one of them learned the other's name.

Will was probably in his late thirties. He sort of looked like the seventies version of Sonny Bono, with the mop of hair looking as if it had been cut with the aid of a soup bowl, and a heavy mustache.

But that was only above the waist. Below the waist, Will sort of looked as if he'd been involved in a three-way collision between himself, a guy who worked at a pizzeria, and Pat Boone! He wore a white T-shirt every day – never so much as a slight color change or anything resembling an emblem on it. And, hidden just slightly behind his mandatory machine-operator's apron was a beer gut that, while not overly obtrusive, was certainly obvious.

However, below the pizzeria T-shirt look, Will always wore a pair of polyester slacks – sometimes green, sometimes maroon, occasionally black – and *always, always, always* topped the ensemble off – or maybe it was more that he *bottomed* it off – with a pair of white, patent-leather shoes.

Oh … and he also always had some sort of heavy gold chain around his neck.

As easy as it might have been for a jeans-and-T-shirt teenager to dismiss this creature as some sort of mutant lounge lizard, the fact was that Chris took a liking to Will almost immediately. For one thing, it was pretty hard *not* to like the guy. He was as close to a pleasant fellow as you ran into at the mill. He seemed to smile most of the time – even if he was up to his gold chain in wayward bobbins and spindles.

Also, Will only worked days, so he got to glad-hand and back-slap with members of both of the alternating shifts.

Finally, you only had to take one look at the guy to see that he was sort of a virtuoso on these machines. Chris often wondered what would happen if every other operator on the floor got food poisoning, and Old Man Blake himself came down and said, "Will, we need you to run every line. Can you do it?"

Chris was pretty sure Will would smile, stroke his Sonny Bono `stache, crack his knuckles, and run up and down the lines, and that production would probably go up that day as a result.

Will usually got to work between five-thirty and six, and hung out in the men's room before the shift began. Chris sometimes wondered if he came right from somewhere other than his home – maybe a poker game, or perhaps a lonely widow's house. He didn't smoke, but no matter what time you go there, Will was already there with one of those little cups of vending machine coffee and a smile.

Chris nodded when he first saw Will, to which the older fellow smiled and said, "Good morning!"

Chris was grateful that Will didn't assume that this was his first day; even though it was his first day shift, he'd worked a week of nights. Then again, Chris learned right away that Will seemed to have a line on just about everything happening on the floor.

"Workin' the big bobbins, eh?" he said with a smile as he took a sip of coffee.

"Uh … yeah," Chris said, surprised that Will knew.

"Good way to make your own way for a while," he said. "Get to work at your own pace, with some of the better people on the line, and you can take your breaks when you want. Too bad you got the floorlady you do."

Chris sighed and nodded.

"Now Molly, the other floorlady, you'd like her. She's pretty reasonable. And Flossie, who was here for many years, she was kind of the same way. This one … Maggie … well, I guess you know about her."

As Will talked, stood there smiling, drank his coffee and seemed oblivious to many problems, Chris wondered how he dealt with Maggie. Since he didn't know him at all, though, he decided not to ask … just yet.

"I guess the key is to just stay ahead of the game, you know?" Will continued. "Don't let things build up to a point where you're swamped. Of course, around noon, with everything rolling, that can get kind of tough. Here's a tip, though. After noon, make one run to get our empty bobbins, then don't worry about the backlog after that. Leave it for the night guy."

Just then, the horn sounded, signaling the start of the shift. Will finished his coffee, tossed the empty paper cup in the trash, and, like some sort of silk-mill Joe Namath jogging out to the huddle, he brashly swaggered out to start his shift, slapping Chris on the shoulder as he passed, exuding the sort of white-shoed confidence, the sort of "hit me with your best shot, Maggie!" élan of which a sixteen-year-old in his second week in the business could only dream.

• • •

A quick meeting with Tony led Chris to a far corner of the floor, where about a dozen pallets stacked with dirty "big bobbins" awaited him. Tony reviewed the procedures quickly – Chris was to take a cart and make as many trips around the floor as possible, picking up used big bobbins that the machine operators left off to the side. Then he had to bring them back to the station and clean them, taking special care to get all the oil off, and finally, he was to take full pallets of clean bobbins, stacked about five high, to the other side of the floor, to a staging area from which a guy named Darrell would collect them and take them down to the second floor, from which they would be sent to be refilled.

After Tony left, Chris spent the next two hours or so doing those tasks for the first time. He managed to clean most of the dirty bobbins left for him by the graveyard shift, and then struggled to get a full pallet to

Darrell's area (eventually, Chris would wonder if Darrell even existed, since nobody he knew had ever seen him).

It was not easy work. The bobbin racks were a lot harder to manipulate than the smaller ones had been. One obvious reason Jeff, for example, couldn't work with them was that the racks were easily nearly six-feet-tall when stacked five high. The taller the bobbin boy, the more potential he had for entering the "big" world.

He took his first break about ten minutes to eight. He wanted to avoid the rush, and given his new position, he didn't necessarily spend his first break with Jeff, Frank, and some of the others he'd been with the week before. One thing he found out was that Richie, the fellow who appeared to be almost crippled, did in fact have some sort of muscular disease, and that he only worked at night.

He was in the men's room by himself for most of his break. Finally, before he was about to leave, Will came in with another machine worker, and then Russell came in. Will exchanged some shop talk with the other worker, but Russell seemed quiet. The atmosphere seemed totally opposite to what it had been at night.

As he left the men's room and returned to his station, Chris glanced at some of the people working on the machines along the way. He noticed one of the women with whom he'd started – the one with the Italian name. He didn't see the other woman. He'd already assumed that Murray, the dim-witted guy who started with them, didn't make it through the first week.

He noticed several other workers along the way. Most of them seemed to be in their forties or even fifties. He wondered if there were any younger people – especially females – on these machines.

When he finally got back near his station, it dawned on him that there was another department adjacent to it. He hadn't noticed it before because the lights were off. But now, after eight, a bizarre, colorful new vista opened up to him, and as he approached his workplace, he sensed that he wasn't alone.

The sixteen-year-old mediocre football player and would-be TV cameraman had a loving and wonderful mother back home. But a kid needs a mother figure on his first job, too, especially if he's been handed such an awesome responsibility as being the "big bobbin boy." On cue, she approached as Chris returned from break. "You must be the new bobbin boy over here!" she said. "Welcome!"

14: A WOMAN'S WORLD

Chris wanted to shake hands with the woman smiling at him, but she didn't have a free hand to shake. She had huge spools of yarn in both her hands, as if she was wearing huge, white boxing gloves.

"This is why I never get to shake hands with anybody!" she giggled, finally freeing her right hand to shake that of Chris. "They say some women always have their hands full, but this is ridiculous!"

Chris smiled and nodded his head politely.

"I guess I should introduce myself," she said. "My name is Shirley. How do you do?"

"Hi ... my name is Chris."

"Well, hello Chris," she said. "Is this your first day at the Blake?"

"Uh ... no," he said. "I worked last week over there ... the small bobbins ... but they told me to come over here today."

"Well, that's great!" she said. "It shows they think you're doing a good job. Some of those guys have been for years and they won't let them work over here."

Shirley was probably in her late forties or even her early fifties, but unlike Frank or Maggie – who looked and acted older than their actual ages – Shirley carried herself like a woman at least ten years younger. In a later time, she would probably be classified as a "MILF," but there was no such classification in the seventies.

She was probably no taller than five-foot-four, but she was in excellent physical shape. She had blond hair with a few streaks of gray, and wore more fashionable glasses than some of the others.

She had on a flowery blouse and pink slacks, with an apron over the blouse. As the Blake had fairly relaxed requirements for footwear, she wore white women's sneakers.

Mostly, though, Shirley wore a smile. But her smile was different from the self-assured smile Will was flashing. When Shirley smiled, it was as if June Cleaver or Harriet Nelson was smiling at you. In fact, one of the first things Chris noticed about her was how out of place she seemed to him among the motley collection of people he'd met so far in this mill.

Shirley worked as a sampler, which meant that she had nothing to do with any of the "dirty work" done on the floor. Shirley had nothing to do with bobbins or pallets; she did not contribute one iota to cacophony on the floor. She only got involved in the process when everything was finished and ready to be packed away and shipped out. She was essentially an inspector of finished products – she literally was the person who put "Inspected by Number Nine" in the box before it went out the door.

Her work area consisted of several thin metal columns on which there were numerous hooks. Because there were samples of all different colors, sizes, and varieties on those hooks, her area tended to look like something from a swinging sixties art gallery, not something in a brick-and-mortar textile mill.

"So Chris," she said, "what ever happened to the other guy they had here? I think his name was Mike."

"I don't know," he said. "I never saw him. Somebody said he quit."

"Well," she said, grabbing another roll from its hook, "that happens a lot around here. I'm sure that bitch Maggie had something to do with it."

Bitch? What happened to June Cleaver? Maggie could turn even a Supermom into a sailor, it seemed.

"It's better working over here, though," she said. "You can pretty much work at your own pace … except when that little witch comes around. That's probably why the other guy quit. She was constantly bothering him."

"It does feel a little cooler over here," he said. "And it's a little quieter."

Shirley stopped and stared at Chris for a moment. She had married children of her own – in fact, her daughter was pregnant with what would be Shirley's first grandchild.

"You must be … what … sixteen or seventeen?" she said.

"Sixteen."

"And you're already getting promoted!" she said before playfully punching him on the arm. "Keep it up, kiddo, and you'll have George's job before long!"

Shirley went back to her work area, and Chris made sure she wasn't watching before he rubbed his arm. It wouldn't have looked right for a kid in high school to admit a middle-aged grandma-to-be had just bruised his arm.

But he knew he liked Shirley, just as he liked Will. They were opposites, to be sure, but they boosted his confidence because they showed him that not everybody at the mill was like George, or Frank, … or especially Maggie!

Maybe Will and Shirley represented the better natures of the older generation at the Blake. He could use a cool faux uncle and a sweet surrogate mother while he was here.

• • •

Chris cleaned bobbins for the next twenty minutes or so, then he noticed Jeff approaching him. He hadn't even seen the group from the small bobbin station since he got in, and he figured maybe Jeff was coming over to say hello.

He was surprised when Jeff approached him somewhat cautiously.

"Uh … Chris," he said. "Can I talk to you for a minute?"

He was so surprised that he actually turned around to make sure there wasn't another Chris nearby.

"Umm ... yeah Jeff ... what's up?"

"Tony wants to see you."

"Tony? The foreman?"

"Yeah, he's over at the desk."

"I wonder what he wants."

Jeff gave Chris an irritated look. "Maybe you're getting another promotion!" he said, obviously with sarcasm.

"What you mean, 'Another one?' This ain't no promotion! I don't get any more money!"

"Yeah, but you don't have to deal with Frank eight hours a day, and you don't have Tony and Maggie standin' right behind you, like we do."

"I guess," Chris said. "Anyway, I'll be right over."

He put his rag in his back pocket and started over toward the middle of the floor, back to where he'd worked the week before, so he could meet with Tony at the foreman's station. He didn't necessarily feel like doing any of this in front of Jeff and Frank and Lawrence, but he didn't have any choice.

He turned the corner and walked past those three en route to talk to Tony, who was leaning against the desk, with his back to everybody else.

But before Chris could approach Tony, he felt a presence moving toward him, and he smelled what he surmised was some sort of World War II-era women's bath powder or body wash – whatever it was, it reeked of *"old lady!"*

"And just where do you think you're going!" scowled the face that only reached up to about his collarbone.

"I'm coming to see ..."

"You're coming to see who?"

"The ... the foreman ... Tony."

"Who told you to come and see the foreman?"

Chris glanced over at Jeff, who had his head down cleaning bobbins. He didn't want to get him involved.

"Somebody told me …"

"What do you mean 'somebody?' Did they have a name?"

Chris looked over at Tony, who was still hunched over the desk. What was his problem? Did he send for him or not? Either way, couldn't he do *something* to get this attack ferret out of his face? Or did they just enjoy seeing her in action?

"You're supposed to be over in the other area!" she snarled. "We can't have bobbins piling up! Don't think that just because you got sent over there that you're something special!"

Not too many years later, what Maggie was doing to Chris would be considered, at least by some, pretty damned close to child abuse. Even though he was almost a foot taller and probably fifty pounds heavier, he still was only sixteen years old.

Chris knew he could give her some lip, come back with a wisecrack, and that she'd probably get twice as ornery. And from what he could tell, there wasn't a soul within earshot who would as much as pick his or her head up to help him out, such was their fear of the shrewish one.

"Just what we needed!" she said. "Another know-it-all cleaning bobbins."

His mind flowed with potential responses. He could:

- Swat her away as if she was a troublesome bee. And get fired.
- Get into a chest-bumping exchange of "Oh yeahs!" with her. And get fired.
- Say something sarcastic, such as, "Yeah, right, I'm such a know-it-all that I decided to come here and clean bobbins for minimum wage!" And get fired.

But what could he really do?

He was a kid. She was an adult. She was an authority figure – a miserable, bitchy, authority one, but an authority figure nonetheless. And she seemed to have all but a few people – including the foreman – scared of her. Finally, she turned to Tony, who was pretending not to have noticed any of it. "Did you want to see him?" she said.

"Yes I did," he said, calmly, as if nothing else had happened.

"All right then," she said, turning back to Chris and pointing at him. "But I'd better not see those bobbins start to pile up! You'd better make all your rounds!"

"Okay," Chris said quietly.

"You'd better make your rounds at least twice after lunch!"

"Okay!" he said more forcefully.

"What did you say?"

"I said 'Okay!'"

She pointed up at him one more time. "You better watch yourself boy!" she said, and she twirled and stormed away.

And then, as if he'd just witnessed nothing more out of the ordinary than a soft breeze blowing through the hallway, Tony oozed away from the desk and toward Chris.

"All right, Tiller," he said. "I wanted to see you because we need you to do something right after lunch … assuming you're caught up after lunch time!"

Chris just shrugged.

"You ever use the elevator before?" Tony asked.

"Elevator? I didn't know we had one!"

"The freight elevator!"

"Uh … no."

"So you don't know the code, then? Shit!"

"The code?"

"Yeah, you need a code to get up there?"

"Up where?"

"Up … well, where you're going. But it don't matter if you don't have the code!"

Chris was wondering if this shift was being run by aliens. He couldn't figure out what Tony was driving at.

"They only person who … oh, shit … never mind! I'll have to call him back."

"Who?"

"Never mind, Tiller!" he barked. Chris wished Tony had used that tone of voice on Maggie while Chris was being sprayed with her spittle. "He ain't gonna give me the code!"

Chris just shook his head. Was Tony drunk or something? What was all this talk about a code? And who was this "he" who was hoarding it?

"Anyway … get your cart after lunch. Make sure it's empty. Go down to the elevator. Wait down there."

"What am I going to do with …"

"Don't worry about it!" Tony barked. "Just take the empty cart right after lunch and wait until the elevator comes down!"

He then dismissed Chris with a wave of his hand. Chris started back to his area when Tony barked at him one more time.

"Tiller!" he yelled. Chris returned and gave him a puzzled look.

"One more thing! For Christ's sake, make sure you've made your God-damned rounds *before* you go to lunch …"

15: FROM THE MOUNTAINTOP

What a way to go to your first ten-in-the-morning lunch! Chris made quick rounds with his cart – as it turned out, only Will had any bobbins for him – and then went off to have his ham sandwich on the edge of the parking lot.

He never was a big fan of eating at cafeteria-style tables with a lot of other people. He tried that one night the week before and found himself sitting next to Lawrence – not a pleasant experience. Between his inane guffawing and the sense that half his food ended up flying out of his mouth, Lawrence was no dining companion. Chris preferred sitting outside by himself.

He thought about his father, who had worked at a metal-processing plant for as long as Chris could remember. Was this what his Dad went through every day? How could you stay sane in that type of environment? Where did these places find people like this, these shrill, sniveling people who treated some stupid building like a dictatorship?

Was it a vestige of the days of coal mining, when overseers whipped breaker boys with sticks if they didn't pick coal fast enough? Had Maggie worked in some old Dickens-era workhouse in a previous life?

And what did they have in mind for him now? What was he going to encounter when he stood at the bottom of that freight elevator? He began to think about whether he really wanted to keep doing this all summer. Sure, he had met some interesting people, people he liked, such as Shirley; or whom he found fascinating, such as Claude and Will.

But to deal with the Maggies of the world? And people like Tony? Or Frank?

Before he knew it, it was half-past noon. He tossed his trash into the wooded area behind the parking lot – everybody did that in those days, although he hadn't been back there yet – and bucked himself up for whatever would come next.

He walked slowly into the mill, up to the third floor, and punched back in. He walked past the elevator. No activity there yet. What if he just stood there now? Without the cart? Would that be some sort of mortal sin?

But there was no doubt what he was going to do. He was going to go get the cart and go back to the elevator. And wait. Really, how bad could it be? If it was any worse than dealing with Maggie, he didn't want to do it; then again, he figured it wouldn't be.

He wheeled the cart around and headed back along the path. It took about a minute to get to the elevator. He waited for at least a few minutes. It was as if the rest of the mill had gone silent; he was so deep in anticipation that he couldn't hear the Lionel engines anymore.

And he heard nothing from the elevator. Moments ticked by, but then, from above, he thought he heard some rumbling. Then it became clearer, and then even clearer than that. The elevator was moving downward, from above, and then it made a thumping sound, signifying that it was coming to a stop.

The next thing Chris knew, there was a noise coming from behind the doors, the sound of metal moving. Then, almost in slow motion, the big metal doors began to open, and the moment was at hand. His rendezvous was at hand, and after a morning in which he'd met Will, and met Shirley, and seen up close what Maggie and Tony could be like, the doors finally opened completely, and Chris looked to see what he would see next.

But the light wasn't on in the elevator, so it was mostly dark. All he saw toward the front was a little cart, much smaller than his own, with what looked to be two jugs on it. He thought he saw a shadow in the darkness behind the cart, but he couldn't tell for sure. But then he heard a voice:

"Well, well," it said. "Who do we have here?"

And then, emerging from the shadow, he saw a man of medium build, probably in his late thirties or early forties, with a dark, full head of hair that didn't appear to have been combed very often in recent days. He was wearing a dark blue work shirt and pants, and steel-toe work boots. He had what looked to be a modest military tattoo on his left forearm, as the long sleeves of his work shirt were rolled up to elbow length.

He was holding a small, pungent-smelling cigar, and his face had stubble on it, as if he had started to develop a five-o'clock shadow sometime around noon.

Chris immediately noticed something on the man's shirt. It was a name patch sewn above his left breast pocket in red lettering on a white oval background. The name was easy to read, even though the man was bent over pushing the small cart:

"Floyd"

The man named Floyd wheeled the cart out into the light, and looked Chris Tiller right in the eye. Chris wasn't sure what to say or do. His mind went blank as he tried to figure out the importance of this man, this meeting, this moment.

But then the man smiled, and had he not said another word, Chris would have realized that this man was no Maggie or Tony. But then again, he wasn't a Will or a Shirley, either.

"Welcome aboard," he said, putting the cigar in his mouth and extending his right hand to shake. "Glad to meet you."

He shook the teenager's hand forcefully yet respectfully. He continued to look him in the eye, as if to reassure Chris that he knew that each was among friends.

"I'm Floyd," he said. "I'm the tester!"

16: ABOVE IT ALL

Chris didn't say much as the tester wheeled the cart out of the elevator, closed the doors, and then motioned to Chris to follow him toward the front of the plant.

"Gotta take these out to get disposed of," he said, pointing to the empty jugs, which Chris figured were designed to hold about fifty gallons of liquid each. "The feds are makin' a big deal about that now. Time was, we just tossed `em with the trash out back. But now they gotta dispose of them through a special process."

Chris nodded as he followed him toward the front. He still didn't know why he'd been sent to meet him, and he sure wasn't certain what the heck a "tester" was. He also was a little concerned that while he was following this guy on a glorified trip to the trash, dirty bobbins would start building up. The period between noon and four was pretty busy on the floor, and Maggie would be looking for him once she saw even a few stray bobbin racks next to her machines.

"So, buddy, what's your name?" the tester said as he wheeled the cart.

"Chris."

"You still in high school, eh, Chris?"

"Yeah … goin' into my senior year."

"Play ball, do ya?"

In this part of the country, "play ball" pretty much meant playing football. Chris had been on the junior varsity team as a junior – which was no accomplishment, since he was one of only three juniors who didn't make it to the varsity. He wasn't totally sure he was even going to try to play again as a senior, figuring that he would never get off the bench even if he did get a uniform, or make the traveling squad.

"Uh-huh," he said. "But I'm not too good."

"Hey, as long as you try, right," the tester said. "I was in the Army for a while, and I spent most of my time cleaning pots, making coffee, picking up trash ..."

He took his right arm off the cart long enough to point to his tattoo.

"Gettin' this ... but then again, they still call me a vet!"

Chris laughed as they approached the area where maintenance workers took out trash and did other related tasks. The tester left the jugs on an area behind a loading bay.

"Probably end up bein' Claude who takes `em out from here," he said. "You meet Claude yet?"

"Oh yeah!" Chris smiled.

Floyd slapped Chris on the shoulder and spun the cart around. Then he threw his palms downward and outward as if to signal to Chris to take the controls, which Chris did.

"Yeah ... high school," he said as they walked. "Enjoy it, whatever the problems are, and however impatient you are to get out. One of these days, you'll say, 'I wish I was still here.' ... Well, not *here*! Not *this* place! I mean high school."

He made a broad gesture with his right hand, as if he was describing the entire mill.

"Hell, in a couple a years, who knows what in the devil's name this place will be!"

They walked slowly back toward the elevator, with Floyd talking all the way.

"So, Tony sent you over here, eh? I guess he probably had to listen to that bag of bones that follows him around."

"Huh?" said Chris.

"That piss bag they have running around on this shift. Don't tell me you ain't run into her yet?"

"Oh, you mean Maggie?"

"Yeah," he said. "She getting on your nerves yet? How long you been here, anyway?"

"A week."

"Well, that's long enough for her to piss anybody off. Especially a bright kid like you. She probably figures if she don't run you outta here, you might end up running the place. You're a bobbin boy, I suppose?"

Chris nodded.

"Yeah," Floyd said. "She likes to boss around the bobbin boys."

They reached the elevator. Floyd stopped, looked at the elevator, and then at Chris, and then he rubbed his chin.

"Hey Chris," he said.

"Yeah?"

"Quick quiz. What's the chemical composition of water? You know, what's the symbol."

Chris was no chemistry major, but he knew the answer to that simple question.

"Symbol … Oh … You mean H-two-oh?"

"Very good! Passed your first chemistry lesson. And … here's the big news. Since you knew that answer, that means you now know the code for the elevator."

"Huh?"

Floyd punched eight-two-one-five into the keypad, and opened the door for the elevator.

"It's a four-number code to run the elevator. 'H' is the eighth letter of the alphabet. Then 'two.' Then the letter 'O,' that's the fifteenth letter of the alphabet. Put 'em together …"

"Eight … two … fifteen?"

"Well .. turn the last number into two …"

"Eight … two … one … five?"

"You got it!" Floyd said. "Fucking George, he's spent half his life trying to figure out that code! And he ain't never gonna figure it out, either!"

He slapped Chris on the back, and the two of them entered the elevator with the cart. Up it went, up two floors to the top floor of the mill, the fifth.

As the doors opened, Chris glanced upon the tester's world of jugs and vats and a variety of other equipment, ranging from teaspoons to complex scientific devices. It looked as if somebody had taken the chemistry classroom at his high school, knocked down a couple of walls, and turned it into an entire wing of the science department.

But mostly, he noticed the smells. Chris grew up near a river that had been heavily polluted by waste products from a nearby paper mill. And his cousins lived a few miles away, near a plant that made creosote. He thought nothing could smell like those places did.

But up here, on the top of the Blake, were smells as pungent as those, and then some. He couldn't imagine having to be around these chemicals even eight hours a day. How could you go home to a wife and children with these fumes all over your clothing? And what would happen to your own sense of smell? He found it hard to imagine ever being able to stop and smell the roses if you've spent forty hours a week surrounded by … by *this*!

On the other hand, though, there was something magical, almost Oz-like, about this top floor and the man who oversaw it. Downstairs, there was all that noise, and with a few exceptions – Shirley, Will, Claude – the workers either had no personality at all, or they had the types of personalities that made Chris wonder how they looked at themselves in the mirror – Tony, George, and especially Maggie.

But up here, this guy, Floyd the tester … well … he just seemed to be above it all, literally and figuratively.

As Chris looked around, he got the impression that Floyd was having a great time just watching him take it all in. His arms folded across his chest, Floyd was standing there, watching him, like a father who had just shown his favorite daughter the new pony he'd just gotten her for her birthday. Chris still wondered why he had been brought up here during the busiest part of the day, but he just sensed that he wouldn't get in any trouble.

He had a feeling he had a new friend, one who would go to the mat for a good bobbin boy.

17: A TIME FOR REVELATION

"So anyway, Chris, how about I tell you a little about myself and this operation up here?"

Chris nodded, and Floyd began the tour, with one arm around the teenager's shoulder, and the other one making grand, sweeping gestures about the surroundings.

"Here's the deal, buddy," he said. "This place … this mill … it has five or six separate departments, any one of them would be a factory by itself in a lot of places. Down on the second floor, there's a big dyeing operation … that's D-Y-E-I-N-G, by the way! I'm down there a lot, but you could probably work on the third floor and never even know they were down there.

"Now on the third floor, you're in the throwing operation. There's some inspecting going on up there … you probably met Shirley, right?"

Chris smiled and nodded that he had.

"Good gal," Floyd said. "Anyway, most of the departments around here, except maybe for what Shirley does, and shipping, I suppose, involve getting textiles …"

He stopped and pointed his right index finger at Chris.

"And don't you ever let me hear you tell anybody you work at a 'silk mill!'" he said. "This ain't the Industrial Revolution here anymore. It's a *textile* mill."

The more Floyd spoke, the more he became "The Tester" in the mind of Chris. But the tester wanted Chris to know a little more about Floyd, too.

"I remember the first time I heard the noise in this place," he said. "I wasn't much older than you. Back then, they still called this place a silk mill … I thought maybe they were working with worms or something in here! Then somebody opened the doors and … *Jee-zus Christ!* Didn't sound like nothing involving silk in here!

"Anyway, like I said, most of what goes on here involves getting textiles ready to be sold all over the world. And what's one thing that could screw up the whole process?"

Chris shrugged.

"Chemicals!" Floyd roared. "God-damned chemicals! They're the key! And I'm the one who has to mix and test all the chemicals that go into all those things they make and twist and whatever the hell else they do down there."

There wasn't much doubt Floyd was working with chemicals. But Chris wondered what made them so important. He didn't have to wonder for long.

"This whole operation would fall apart if I didn't do my job right," Floyd said. "Without the proper chemical levels, the whole operation goes down."

He reached for a device that had been placed on a table. It looked like a big rubber straw with a bulb – not a light bulb, but the kind of bulb on the back end of a turkey baster – attached to it. The closest thing Chris had ever seen to this device was something his father used to use to try to test the anti-freeze in his car radiator.

"Watch this!" Floyd said. He placed the open end of the straw into a small, rectangular receptacle on the table, into which he poured some fluid. Then he removed the bulb-like device and literally blew bubbles into the fluid.

"I use this to test the solutions they soak some of the materials in," he said. "They have to have the proper chemical compatibility and consistency, you know?"

Chris was beginning to wonder something about this man who called himself "the tester." To look at him, the tester was a typical working man; he could have easily passed for a mechanic, or maybe a laborer at the plant where Tom Tiller worked. And he had sort of a down-to-earth personality. He certainly didn't seem like some sort of scientist, but he seemed to have the knowledge of one.

"I'm surprised they put you over on the big bobbins by yourself," the tester said. "You must be what, eighteen or so?"

"Sixteen," Chris said.

"Sixteen!" the tester yelled. "Damn! You have many run-ins with George yet?"

"Kinda," Chris said. "The first night I was here, he caught me sitting on one of the sinks in the men's room. I mean, I didn't know you weren't supposed to do that … I can see his point, I guess, but …"

"George!" the tester interrupted. He shook his head and started to chuckle as he walked away. Then he turned around, and Chris could sense that the tester had a few opinions on the subject of the superintendent.

"Let me tell you about George," he said. "George knows a little more than most folks about some of the machinery. He's been here a long time and he has put in some hours to learn about it. He's not lazy, and he knows his shit … such as it is.

"But he has a problem with authority … he thinks he *is* the authority! If there's one thing that son-of-a-bitch has been doing since the day I met him it's been kissing up to the owners. He rode that all the way to the superintendent's job, and he took that little Maggie with him as far as they'd let him.

"But there's one thing George most certainly does *not* know … and that's the fuckin' chemistry! And he doesn't know shit about what I do! He acts like he knows it all, but he couldn't do this job. And there was a time when they wanted him to."

"George?" said Chris.

"Oh yeah. Before I even knew what was going on. I just got outta the service and came back here for a job."

"You worked here before?"

"Oh yeah, just like you. For one summer before I went in the service. But anyway, I came back and unbeknownst to me, George was pushing to get this job that I have now."

"So how did you get it?"

The tester smiled and motioned for Chris to sit down. He went and got two cups of coffee, both black.

"Don't know how you take it, so I figured we'd start with black," he said. Chris, who didn't drink coffee much, nodded and started to sip the black coffee, which, to his surprise, wasn't that bad.

"So before I tell you about how I got here, let's talk about where you're going. You got one more year of school, I suppose."

Chris nodded.

"Then what, off to college?"

"If I can."

"Yeah, well, it'd keep you outta Vietnam, eh? Can't say I blame you. I was in Korea, you know, but this Vietnam … rough shit. Well, let's hope it's over soon … but anyway, what I meant was, what you going to study?"

"I don't know, maybe accounting," he said. He felt embarrassed to suggest he wanted to work in television. "My brother does that. Maybe engineering."

The tester got up and started to walk around. He pointed to the floor.

"You know, I used to be down there," he said, referring to the third floor. "One summer … started as a bobbin boy. Just like Andrew Carnegie!"

"Andrew Carnegie?" Chris said. "You mean the millionaire? The one they named Carnegie Tech after?"

"That's right," the tester said. "He was a bobbin boy, you know? In Scotland or someplace. And he became, you know, the richest man in the world!"

The tester mussed up Chris's hair.

"So I did that one summer, then after I graduated from high school the next year, I went in the service. Couple of years later, I came home and was kinda desperate for a job, so I came back up here. I was figuring I'd be a bobbin boy again, or maybe work one of the machines, ya know? But the day I showed up, for Christ's sake, there was a big scene in the office. One of the big shots, whose name I can't remember, and then Artie, who was the superintendent before George. They're in a big argument with this other guy in a lab coat.

"From what I was told, part of the argument was that they wanted George to work with this fellow in the lab coat. But it turned out, this fellow hated George's guts, and there I was, standin' there, so they picked me instead."

"Who was he?" said Chris.

The tester stood directly in front of him and looked him in the eye.

"Chris ... it was the *chemist.* You know, the guy who taught me all this!"

"Was he really a chemist?"

"Oh yeah!" he said. "He went to some school in Philly and was some kinda big shot in the Army during the war. One time, I made a joke that he had invented the bulletproof vest. He chewed me out and told me never to joke about that again!"

"Sounds like he was an impressive guy," Chris said.

"Well, keep in mind, I wasn't all that much older than you are now, and here they picked me outta the blue to work with this guy who taught me all the tricks of making sure everything they did here was chemically correct. See, he knew that they didn't know their ass from a hole in the ground when it came to the chemistry. He knew that the government would eventually shut them down once he left … nobody here knew what the hell was going on! So he wanted to train somebody to take over. But they were too cheap to hire another chemist, and … well, there I was, standin' there, that day!"

"That's amazing," Chris said.

"It took me about a year to learn all the ins and outs, you know?" the tester said. "After that, he'd come by once a month or so for about another year … he used to come over from New York, where he lived. By the time I stopped working with the chemist, there wasn't anybody in this place … from old man Blake on down … who knew as much about the chemistry, and who was as crucial to keeping this place in business, as me.

"Of course … that don't include the chemist himself!"

"Oh, of course not," said Chris.

"The other thing the chemist taught me was not to take any shit from those people down there," the tester said. "In fact, to this day, whenever George or Maggie try to tell me anything about my job, I tell them to get lost, and I say 'I learned this from the chemist, where did you learn it?' That really pisses them off!"

"Too bad I can't say that!" Chris said.

The tester gave him a playful punch on the arm.

"Well, maybe you can, in a way," he said. "Here's the deal. You're on that fucked-up schedule, right? One week days, one week nights?"

"Yeah."

"Okay … so every week when you're working days, no matter what Miss Prissy says or has you do … or for that matter, even if George has you washing his fucking car … when I come down and get you, you stop what you're doing and you come up with me. Bring your cart. We'll take some of these jugs, which are filled with chemicals that you don't want to spill, down there, and I'll do my job, and we'll get the empty jugs and bring them back up here."

"As long as they don't mind," Chris said.

"It don't matter if they don't mind!" the tester replied tersely. "My work comes first. This is an important job, Chris! If you jostle these chemicals, you could not only burn yourself pretty badly, but cause some sort of industrial spill that might shut the plant down. You gotta make sure you don't jostle 'em!"

"No jostlin'!" he said.

"And as far as that little ... that little bitch is concerned ... well, you can't tell her you learned it from the chemist, right?"

"No, guess not."

"But you can do the next best thing," he said. "Tell her you're under orders from the tester."

Chris smiled. The thought of doing that very thing was too magnificent to even dream about. But he relished it nonetheless.

"Okay!" Chris laughed.

By now, they were done with their coffee. The tester threw his cup in the trash and sat down next to Chris.

"Anyway, Chris, I asked for you because you kind of remind me of me when I first started here. Bobbin boy, good head on your shoulders. This job will get you away from those losers down there ... Frank and those guys ... and give you a little experience with some of the other things that go on around here. I mean, I don't expect you to end up in this business like I did, but at least when you go on to college, you'll have done more than just wipe oil off bobbins and listen to Maggie piss and moan."

The tester pulled a cigar out of his vest pocket and lit it. Chris was surprised to see him do that, given that they were surrounded by chemicals. But he figured the tester knew what he was doing.

"You know, Chris, I don't know how long I would have worked down there ... if I hadn't come up here, I mean," he said, pointing to the floor again. "I couldn't take working for George. I'd have popped him eventually.

"The thing is, I could go work for Union Carbide or DuPont or one of those companies, ya know?" he said. "I don't have a degree or anything, but the chemist, he was always a big deal in the industry. His name carried a lot of weight. Still does. I've had offers …"

The tester wandered over about halfway to where the elevator was. He began to stare at the elevator, but Chris sensed that he was really staring off beyond those doors. Something was obviously on his mind, and Chris got the impression that he was the person to whom it was finally going to be revealed.

"You know, Chris, these places are all gonna be empty before too long …"

Chris wasn't sure what he meant.

"What places?" he said.

"This place … Rogers, over on the West Side … the United mill off by the highway," the tester said. He was naming some of the town's other textile mills.

"This … this whole … this whole industry … it can't last. Not the way it has been."

When the tester said that, Chris thought about all the factories in his town. They had once been all over the place. Some were small, family-owned operations, places where they made shoes or other small consumer items such as that, places with maybe a dozen steady workers.

Others were pretty big. His father's plant must have had a hundred workers. There was a shirt factory right near his house, and they ran two full shifts, employing at least that many workers, most of them women.

And the mills he mentioned, they were even larger. The Rogers mill probably had at least as many workers as the Blake, and the building itself was definitely bigger – seven floors, he figured. It occupied at least a city block on the West Side, and when you threw in the parking areas and the train tracks nearby, it was almost like a town in itself. It was famous for its huge clock, with a large statue of a golden eagle perched on top of it. You could see the clock – and the eagle – from half a mile away.

What would all those workers do if those places closed? And where would their jobs go? Wouldn't *somebody* have to make those shoes, and those shirts, and those yarns? The thought of those jobs just being sent somewhere else ... well, it didn't occur to too many people in 1971.

"The people here, they really don't think about the future," the tester said. "But I do. I think about it a lot. The chemist ... he told me once 'Don't ever think that the next big thing is the last big thing!' It's like a general fighting the last war. You have to think one, two moves ahead. The people who run these factories around here ... they only know one way, and that's how they always did it."

He took a puff on his cigar and walked back toward Chris.

"It's a good thing you're not here permanently," he said to Chris. "You'd be out of a job in ... I don't know ... ten, maybe twenty years."

The tester chuckled as he realized what he said.

"Listen to me, tellin' a sixteen-year-old about workin' here in twenty years!" he said. "You don't even know what twenty years are yet! But the thing is, there are people your age down there ... you know, some of those jerk-offs they got workin' down there, those pot-heads or whatever you wanna call 'em ... and they don't have any plan for their lives, so they'd just stay here, I guess, if they could. But they ain't gonna be able to do that. They're gonna be thirty-five years old and out of a job, and not a thing to fall back on!

"These places ... these factories around here ... look how old they are! Half of `em ain't had a decent coat of paint in twenty years! They're fucking relics! Nineteenth-century relics. They're gonna be ghost towns by the time you know it! Naw, Chris. Don't you get stuck in here!"

"I'm not planning to," Chris said.

The tester smiled. Chris got the sense the tester was happy to see that his warning to Chris seemed to have gotten through. But he also sensed that the tester was unhappy because ... well ... because he believed he was right about the fate of the mill to which he'd devoted his life, and of the industrial base on which the town in which he'd spent that life had been built.

He had the feeling that even if he was the first young man to whom the tester would spread this message, he would not be the last. He expected that just as the chemist had prepared him for his life in the mill, he would spend summer after summer preparing young men like Chris for the realization that, in all probability, there would be no life in this mill … and maybe in this town … for them.

He would leave it to them to figure out if they were better or worse off as a result.

"Good boy!" the tester said when Chris responded to him. "I'm just trying to pass things along, you know? The chemist passed a lot along to me. I'm passing it along to you. Someday, pass it along to some other kid … in whatever job and whatever town you find yourself. Okay?"

Chris nodded his head. Part of him wished he could go out and spread the word right away … but he had some growing up to do first!

"So I'll come get you whenever we need to transfer the chemicals," the tester said. "It don't matter what you're doing; you come with me. And remember, no …"

"No jostling!"

"That's right!" the tester said. "And what if Maggie gives you a hard time?"

The sixteen-year-old thought about it.

He usually didn't speak his mind in front of adults, and certainly watched his language in front of them. But then again, had he ever been around an adult like this before?

He began to speak, and the volume and timbre of his voice rose with each word, until the final four words burst out of his mouth with the sort of enthusiasm one usually hears from a revival-tent preacher, or a sledgehammer-wielding used car salesman on a late night television commercial.

"I'll tell her," he said. *"To go fuck herself!"*

18: A CHANCE ENCOUNTER

A week went by, then another, and Chris spent a lot of his time on the floor ducking Maggie and helping out the tester.

One day, he was helping out upstairs right after lunch on the day shift. When Chris finally got back down to the third floor, it was nearly time for the noon break. The floor was running at almost full capacity, and there were racks of dirty bobbins everywhere.

Had he run into Maggie as soon as he got off the elevator, there might have been a scene. But she was involved in some minor crisis on the other side of the floor, so he didn't run into her right away.

He knew he couldn't just go right on his break; he had to get some of those bobbins off the floor. He wasn't concerned about cleaning them – the night crew could handle that – but he had to get them picked up. So he walked quickly back to his station and grabbed his cart.

He figured the best thing to do would be to work on the half of the floor farthest away from his station. So he bypassed the stacks nearest to him and went over to clear out the buildup on the other side.

That took him about ten minutes, and he managed to keep a wide berth between himself and Maggie. If she complained, he could say that he had been busy on that side.

He brought the load of racks to his station and carefully maneuvered them on to a pallet. He decided to wait a minute until he started to pick up the bobbins closest to him.

There were two issues worrying him as he plotted his strategy. First, where was Maggie?

Second, he knew that the prodigious Will had probably used up a week's worth of bobbins by now. Fortunately, he figured that Will would realize he was doing something else, and would not just pile his used bobbins up on the floor so that Maggie would see them.

He turned his cart around and started gathering more racks. He picked up four racks on two machines, and had his head down as he approached a third machine. He wasn't really looking where he was going, and as he went to pick up the empty rack from the third machine, he noticed that somebody was putting another rack out for him.

He looked up to see who it was.

She had green eyes. Well, they were sort of green, with a touch of blue in each of them. He'd never looked so closely into somebody's eyes before. As he pulled his gaze back from them, he saw the rest of her face. She had a round face, with smooth, milky white skin. She was wearing a blue bandana, but underneath it, Chris could see auburn hair, cut somewhat short for the time, but still falling well to her shoulders.

She looked to be in her late teens, and she was the first girl he'd seen on the floor who was even close to his age. She was wearing jeans, a dark T-shirt, and the mandatory apron. She had on clogs, which were popular among young women in 1971, and striped socks.

Her figure … well, it was a bit chubby, but not in an unattractive way. Her bustline was as large and well-developed as he had ever seen on someone that age. So, to a sixteen-year-old who had not yet had a girlfriend, who had bungled away a half-dozen opportunities to even ask girls at school out on dates, and who had not really come close to losing his virginity, this lovely creature surely was an incredible contrast to the battlewagons, large and small, he'd seen elsewhere in the plant.

And then she smiled at him. Who knew that someone like this could smile at him? With the Lionels chugging, and the floorlady ready to pounce, and the racks stacking up elsewhere … she smiled at him.

"Uh … thanks!" was all he could say.

She tilted her head slightly, kept smiling, and turned and walked away. He watched her walk slowly, provocatively, as she disappeared into another part of the mill. His mind racing, he turned back toward his station and emptied the few racks he'd just collected onto a waiting pallet. Then he stood there, his cart empty, oblivious to everything as he stared back toward where the girl had been.

Shirley, having noticed that his load had been light, approached him, yarn in each hand.

"Busy Chris?" she said.

"Huh?"

"I said, 'Busy Chris?'"

"Uh … oh … yeah … sorry … I … I … just …"

Shirley giggled.

"I noticed."

"Huh?"

"Are you distracted, Chris?"

"Uh … no … but … Hey, Shirley?"

"Yes?"

"Mind if I ask you something?"

She had a feeling what he was going to ask.

"No, go ahead."

"Do you know … uh … what her name is?"

"Who?" she said, even though she had a good idea.

"That girl."

"The one who was just over here? With the bandana?"

"Yeah."

"Why … you got a crush on her or something?"

"No!" he said, turning red. "I just wondered what her name is."

Shirley shrugged and walked a few steps to put down her yarn. "I … To be totally honest, Chris, I really don't know."

"You don't?"

"No," she said. "I guess she's been here about six months. She never talks to anybody. I thought I heard Tony call her Mary once … but I'm really not sure. Sorry!"

"That's okay," he said. "Does she ever talk to Maggie?"

Shirley's eyes picked up as if she realized something. "To be honest, I've seen Maggie try to talk to her a couple of times, but I never heard her yell at her or anything. And I can't remember her saying anything back. As I recall, Maggie got frustrated and left. Like I said, I've never heard her say anything."

"Hmmph," Chris said.

"Are you sure you're not sweet on her?"

"You mean on Maggie?" Chris joked.

"Oh … *yuck!*" Shirley said. "No, I mean on that girl over there!"

"No … I just wondered …"

"She is kinda cute, isn't she Chris?"

Before Chris could answer, he heard the sound of a cart approaching. He turned, and the tester was next to him. The tester looked at Shirley and they both smiled.

"What we got going on here?" he said.

"I'm just helping Chris with his love life," Shirley said.

"I see," the tester said. "Well, don't tell his mother … we'll all be in trouble!"

Chris sensed that Shirley and the tester were friends … if not more. He noticed that both wore wedding rings, but through his brief stint at the mill, he noticed that plenty of flirting went on, wedding rings or no wedding rings. Most of it was probably innocent, but he figured some of it probably was not. If there was anything between these two, he didn't want to know; he already had enough on his mind.

"So, there, young man, who is it you have the crush on?" the tester said.

Shirley whispered something in the tester's ear.

"Oh, her!" the tester said. "You know, I've never heard her say a word. She's been here … I don't know, at least about what, six months? Never heard her open her mouth. She's quieter than you!"

"Me?" Chris said.

"Yeah. But then again, I've never heard anything bad about her."

While he was listening to the tester, Chris noticed that Maggie was lurking off about twenty feet away. Chris had never seen her lurk like that. Usually, it seemed, when she had a notion, she would burst over to let loose on her victim. There was no doubt she had her eye on Chris; she couldn't have missed the bobbins stacking up even as he, Shirley, and the tester talked.

But something seemed to stay Maggie's hand … not to mention her ire. And the tester … well, he knew what it was, and he was going to keep staying.

"So …" he said, drawing out the word. "Shirl … don't you think she … what is that gal's name, anyway?"

Shirley, who had daily run-ins with Maggie, was more than willing to keep the tester around.

"I don't know, really," she said, also talking more slowly. "I thought I heard somebody call her Mary …"

"Can't say for sure myself," the tester said. "But I'm pretty sure she works over in packing sometimes, too. And I think she's about your age, Chris."

The three of them laughed, and as they did, Maggie seethed. Even the slightest sign of joviality on the floor usually sent her into a rage, but though Chris could practically sense her blood pressure climbing, he noticed that she didn't move.

"He needs to get a girlfriend at school this year, don't you think?" said the tester to Shirley.

And that was it! The brain of Maggie O'Hara couldn't take any more. It told her to motor her little body over there and break up this three-way gabfest, to go through it like a plow through a fluffy January snowfall.

But somewhere else in there was the memory of every other time something like this had happened, ever since the day that damned chemist with the damned lab coat took that kid upstairs and turned him into the God-darned untouchable sacred cow that the little Irish wench couldn't lay into … lest she wanted to be one ex-floorlady.

"Umm … aren't there some bobbins that need to be picked up?" she said as she sidled up to Chris. He sensed venom in her voice, that of a cobra who wanted to spit at its victim, but realized that somebody had just milked the poison dry.

"I just did some rounds," Chris said. "I'll get the others before I go."

"And look at these piling up!" she said. "I bet you figure you'll just leave them for the night shift! Well, let me tell …"

"Actually, he has some work to do for me!" the tester interrupted. "Chris, why don't you make a quick run for some more bobbins, then meet me over at forty-two. You know where that is?"

"Forty-two?" he said. "Is that … one of those machines on the other end?"

"Yeah," Maggie said. "It's the one with number 'forty-two' on it."

"Right," the tester said, glaring at her. "They figured that out around here without any training … isn't that amazing? Meet me at forty-two!"

Shirley slinked away to her area. She figured she should avoid Maggie the rest of the day.

"You get this done first!" Maggie screeched, pointing to the racks of dirty bobbins.

"I have some *important* work to do over there!" the tester roared back. "Chemisty work."

Chris felt as if he was now part of a clash of wills. He knew Maggie wasn't going to back down, and that she would continue to press him to get the bobbins. But he also knew that the tester was not going to let her get the upper hand on him. Who, he wondered, would fire the final, winning salvo?

"Meet me there!" he said to Chris.

"You get this done first!" Maggie screeched at Chris, pointing to the bobbins. Then she turned to the tester, gritted her teeth, stared him in the eyes, and took her shot.

"And who said we needed anything done on forty-two?" she snarled.

"I did," he said, glaring back at her.

"That's my responsibility!" she said.

Chris looked at the tester. He noticed that he wasn't trying to physically intimidate Maggie; almost anybody in the mill could do that. He realized that the tester had to defeat Maggie on her level, had to match her scowl for scowl, sarcasm for sarcasm, glare for glare.

Chris wondered what, if anything, the tester had left in his arsenal.

The tester put his hands on his hips. He stared at Maggie and spoke directly, but not angrily. He would have to rely on what he said, not how he said it, to defeat this adversary yet again.

"I am responsible for the chemistry in this mill," he said directly. "There is an issue on forty-two."

He looked Maggie in the eyes, and as he spoke, Chris could almost sense the power of his words; it was as if Thor had unleashed his hammer, or as if The Thing had decided it was clobberin' time.

"And so … *Margaret* … let me do my job!"

When Chris heard those three syllables … *"Mar-gar-et"* … it was as if he'd seen a house fall on a wicked witch. Maggie didn't melt away or anything, but he could see her face twist into a horrific scowl. She was beaten … again. Chris had no idea how many times this scene had played out in the previous years at the Blake, but he was sure this hadn't been the first time.

Maggie huffed and stormed away, and the tester chuckled and nodded his head.

"You better get all those bobbins before you go," he said to Chris. "She'll be even more pissed off at you tomorrow if you don't."

And then the tester took his cart and went back upstairs. Chris got his cart and began collecting bobbins. He looked off toward where he knew the packing area was, where the girl might be working. He couldn't see her from where he was, but from that day on, there would be very few moments during his time at the mill when he wouldn't think about her.

19: ANDY AND CAROL

Even after every confrontation with Maggie, Chris never really thought about quitting his job. He just wondered whether any amount of money was worth being around Maggie and her misery.

He was just starting to develop an understanding for what made people act the way they did. He hadn't given it much thought until recently – before a boy turns sixteen, he rarely even thinks about anybody but the members of his family and perhaps a few close friends. But in the months leading up to the end of his junior year in high school, he started to wonder why people behaved the way they did.

What made some kids walk through the halls of the high school as if they were crown princes strolling through some medieval town?

Why did others seem to drift through the hallways, as if they didn't exist?

And why was it that one chubby girl would seem to have dozens of friends, of both genders, while some other chubby girl was lucky to find anybody else to talk to?

Then there were the adults … and they were no better! Some teachers might as well have been part of the student body, what with how they joked around and hung out with students in the hallways.

But there were others, who were no less educated, no less experienced, and they ended up getting their houses egged at Halloween, got crank phone calls every weekend, and had curses about them scratched in the desktops of their classrooms.

Why was that?

He had begun to think about people at the mill that way. How come that girl never talked to anybody? What put her on one end of the spectrum, while somebody like Will, who never seemed to stop talking to people, was on the other end?

But mostly, he wondered about Maggie. He'd come across women like her before – spinster schoolteachers, crazy aunts, ornery nuns. What made them that way? Hadn't they once been playful little girls, running around in the grass, or helping their mothers cook dinner on Thanksgiving? Didn't they get dressed up on Easter and go to church wearing little bonnets, smiling as the newspaper photographers snapped photos of them?

What was it, he wondered, that turned a little boy into a bully, or turned a little girl into a … a Maggie? There had to be something.

He was kicking that around in his mind when he heard a man's voice:

"Here comes the hard-working fellow now!"

Chris looked up and smiled. He saw a man in his forties, accompanied by a woman perhaps a few years younger. He'd seen them before, and they always exchanged pleasantries with him, but all he really knew about them was that he'd never seen either one without the other.

The woman tilted her head slightly to look at Chris. She seemed concerned for his welfare.

"Are you doing okay?" she said.

Although the sixties had come and gone, these two seemed to have skipped most of the crazy stuff people would later associate with that decade.

The man, whose name was Andy, wore his hair short, and was still using Brylcreem or Vitalis or something to slick it back. He did have sideburns, extending down to about his earlobes. He wore dark-rimmed glasses

– he hadn't gotten to wire rims yet – and had on a light, button-down, short-sleeved shirt. He had on khaki slacks and black shoes.

In short, he looked like what many people in 1971 would still have called a "square."

Carol, the woman, wasn't exactly a hippie chick either. She was a little chubby, and at about five-foot-three, she was only about four inches shorter than Andy. Chris was already taller than either of them.

Carol wore her hair in a style that probably would have fit very nicely into a 1968 high school yearbook – it was something along the lines of what Sally Field's hair looked like in the TV show "Gidget." Her blouse was light, with a flowered pattern, and she had on dark slacks and black flat shoes. She was dressed for nothing but a few hours of factory work.

Andy and Carol both worked on throwing machines, but Chris noticed that neither wore an apron. In fact, he had never seen either of them actually doing anything on a machine – it was as if they disappeared somewhere, and their work magically got done. They always had used bobbins near their stations, as they did during this run.

"Maggie wearing you down?" said Andy, his smile indicating that he already knew the answer.

"She's just … she's just *ridiculous!*" Chris blurted out.

Carol's expression, which had been one of concern, turned to one of anger.

"What a bitch!" she said.

Andy laughed as he and Carol exchanged looks.

"Hey buddy," he said to Chris. "She does that to everybody."

"Yeah," said Carol. "But she doesn't have to be such a … such a *bitch* about it! I mean, you can get things done and still be civil to people!"

"Civil?" Andy said. "I don't think she can be civil!"

Chris was going to respond, but he noticed that Andy and Carol were looking at each other as if they knew a secret.

"I can't imagine what she must be like outside of this place," Andy said, as both of them nodded their heads.

"Maybe she's a sweet little lady who helps all the kids in the neighborhood!" said Chris. He had already put Andy and Carol's used bobbins on his cart, and he was just trying to make a joke.

"Oh I don't know!" said Carol, failing to pick up on the sarcasm. "I don't think she's like that at all!"

"I think our boy was just kidding!" Andy said.

Carol giggled, finally getting the joke. But then she got serious again.

"I just can't stand her!" she said.

Andy and Carol shared that "we-know-a-secret" look again. Andy then took his eyes off Carol briefly and turned to Chris.

"The thing is, you gotta just shut her up. And you do that by beating her at her own game. She's gonna be looking for you … when?"

"Uh … maybe right after I come back …"

"Right!" he interrupted. "Right after lunch. Right after your break. And right before quitting time. Make sure she sees you picking up bobbins. Even if it's just a few. If she sees you picking up bobbins, she can't give you a hard time. Or at least she won't make a big scene about it."

Chris nodded his head. Then he had a thought. For a sixteen-year old, it was a bit audacious.

"Either that," he said. "Or I could call her Margaret!"

Andy and Carol grimaced almost in unison. They were impressed! This kid had picked up a lot of inside dirt in his short time in the mill!

"Honey," Carol said, putting her hand on his arm, "if you do that, you can stop by and pick up my bobbins anytime!"

Andy and Carol then laughed together, almost on cue, and headed back to wherever they worked. Chris noticed that as they departed, Andy gingerly put his right hand on Carol's back.

He watched them disappear. Then he realized he wasn't far from "forty-two," the machine where the tester had said he would be working. He rolled his cart about twenty feet, and there was the tester, kneeling down and using that device he had shown Chris, the one he used to test the chemicals.

He had the tube end in a tray underneath the throwing arms, a tray where the chemicals were poured and mixed, and from which they were distributed into the machine to be absorbed into the textiles.

The tester also had what looked like a straw. He blew bubbles of air into the chemicals through his straw, then he used the bulb on the other end of the device to blow air in through the tube. He repeated this process a few times, each time writing something on a small note pad he had with him.

Chris watched as he did this. There was something about watching this gruff man, in work clothes, literally blowing bubbles, that seemed almost surreal to him. When the tester went to work, it was as if the rest of the mill went silent, as if the concentration the tester brought to his efforts was somehow transmitted to his young assistant, who though he knew nothing about the chemical aspect of it, could tell that whatever the tester was doing somehow ascended high above what anybody else in the building was doing.

"Not bad," the tester said. "Good enough to last a while."

He noticed that Chris was looking at him, so he stood up, holding his devices in one hand, and he smiled.

"Hey Chris!" he said. "Ready to go bring some more chemicals down here?"

"Well, I'm supposed to be …"

"Hey!" the tester interrupted. "What's the first rule?"

"Don't jostle `em?"

The tester laughed. "Well, there's that, too! But the first rule is, when I say I need you to help me with the chemicals, then that's what you do. And Maggie can go … well, you know what she can do."

Chris smiled, and the tester patted him on the shoulder and motioned for him to walk with him to the elevator.

"Hey, can I ask you something?" Chris said when they got there.

"Yeah, what's up?" the tester said.

"Those two over there," Chris said, pointing back to where he'd been speaking to Andy and Carol. "Andy and …"

"Carol?"

"Yeah … Carol …"

The tester smiled and looked him in the eye. He waited for a few seconds before responding.

"You wanna know why they're always together, huh?"

Chris nodded.

"You noticed that, huh?"

"Well, yeah," Chris said. "Are they … are they married or something?"

"Yes … and yes," the tester said with a shrug.

"Huh?"

"Well, I know Andy's married anyway …"

Chris was confused at first, but then he figured out what the tester was implying.

"Oh … you mean … you mean they're married … but …"

"Right!" the tester said. "Not to each other!"

Chris felt embarrassed. He was old enough to know about some things, but he was still only sixteen, and he sure didn't know about *everything!*

"Hey, that's the way it is in here, bud!" the tester said as the elevator doors opened. "My wife thinks I'm screwin' around with half the gals in here …"

He pointed his right index finger at Chris.

"I'm not, by the way," he said. "But hell, who am I talkin' to here? Look at you. You only been here a little while, and you already got your eye on that gal with the bandana over there!"

"Who said that?" Chris said, even more embarrassed now. "I didn't say anything …"

"I didn't say anything!" said the tester, imitating Chris. "You ain't got to say it, bud. Folks like me … Shirley … you know, we been around. Sorry to tell you, bud, but it's all over your face. I think you're in love!"

Chris felt as if his face was on fire. The tester took his right hand and wrapped it around the bobbin boy's chin, pinching his cheeks together and laughing.

They got on the elevator, and it took at least a half-hour before the tester stopped teasing him about the girl with the bandana, and before Chris Tiller's face reverted to room temperature.

20: A TALE OF TWO TEENS

The summer of 1971 raced by, and once the long month of July ground toward its conclusion, Chris Tiller knew he was getting closer to ending his time at Blake Textiles.

For most of his life, July meant hanging around with his friends, with a usual weeklong interlude with his family at the Jersey Shore. Going to the shore was a ritual practiced by many families in his town, and each trip had been one of the highlights of his life right through the end of the sixties.

But for some reason – Chris assumed it had to do with money – the family hadn't gone the summer before. So he had spent all of the previous July just hanging around, bouncing between this candy store and that five-and-dime. He'd done a little swimming, and they'd played a lot of sandlot baseball. But there had been a definite void, and when 1971 came around, he knew as he began to look for a job that he probably wouldn't be going back to the seaside for a while.

So July was just a long month, one week of working days, one week of working nights. That was followed by one week of days, and one week of nights. The paychecks were nice, and he bolstered his record collection with the latest by the Rolling Stones and The Who, but he began to understand just why his father and other adults referred to their daily trips to work as "the grind."

Life at the Blake as summer wore down was more or less routine. He helped the tester, tried to avoid Maggie, did what Tony said to do, joked with Shirley, and stopped to talk to Andy and Carol when he could.

But he never said a word to the girl in the bandana. As August got underway, he wondered if he would ever hear her speak.

They had exchanged glances, and even smiles. Chris thought he saw a gleam in her eye when she saw him looking at her, and he wondered if he thought there was one in his. But he just was not sufficiently equipped at that point in his life to approach her out of the blue.

He thought about it often, and if anything gave him incentive to get up at five in the morning if he was on the day shift, or to leave his house at one in the afternoon if he was working nights, it wasn't the money he was making, or the albums he could buy. It was the possibility that this might be *the day;* would they actually speak, or would he at least learn her name?

But it never was. And so, on the first Monday in August, he left the house at one in the afternoon for a slow walk to Blake Textiles. A healthy teenager could actually make the walk in thirty to forty minutes, but Chris often liked to stop at the store on the way.

Whenever he walked to work in the afternoon before a night shift, Chris passed by the school with the outdoor basketball courts – the one with the television station in the basement.

From September to June, if you went past the school around mid-morning, or mid-afternoon, you'd see a gaggle of the school's students out flailing away with basketballs during gym classes.

After school hours, however, and on weekends – and, especially, in the summer – the courts were taken over by just about anybody else in town who wanted to play basketball. There were eight hoops in all, making up four full courts. Games were almost always of the half-court variety, so on a busy day, there would be eight games going on, anywhere from two-on-two to five-on-five.

Depending on the time of day, the players could be of elementary school age, dreaming perhaps of playing for the school someday, or they could be adults out for some pick-up play after work.

It didn't take much to get a game going. If you had a ball, you just started shooting at the first available basket. If somebody was already there, you just shot around them. The protocol of the playground ruled. If you made your shot, somebody would rebound and get your ball back to you. If you missed, then somebody else would get the ball and take a shot. It was unspoken, and it worked to perfection.

When Chris was walking home from work after the day shift, he was usually too tired to think about shooting hoops. But when he was walking to work for a night shift, he usually envied the kids who were able to just spend their summers playing basketball instead of working. More than once, he had to put his head down and walk quickly past the courts, lest he be too tempted to get in a game.

He did this through most of July, and then, one day in early August, he was walking to another night of bobbin cleaning.

Walking to work in the middle of a summer afternoon was never pleasant. It was much more fun to walk home after a day shift, when he could take his time, stop at a corner store, and think about what he was going to do the rest of the night – maybe a trip downtown to the record store, or perhaps a trip with some of his buddies to a pizza joint. There wasn't all that much to do in town during the summer, but it beat being stuck in a textile mill at night. But having to walk *to* work was drudgery.

On that August day, he made a quick stop at a store for a sixteen-ounce bottle of Pepsi. In those days, Pepsi, like all brands of soda pop, came in heavy, glass bottles, for which one paid a slight deposit – a few cents at most. Nothing before or since – no metal, plastic, paper, or any other container – duplicated the taste of a soft drink from those bottles.

But Chris certainly wasn't thinking of that as he drank from his Pepsi bottle that day while approaching the basketball courts. He was just about finished drinking from it when he looked up and saw a familiar figure approaching him on the sidewalk from the other direction.

"Hey Chris," the teenager said. "What's up?"

Chris smiled as he approached the young man, who was wearing a tight, white T-shirt, light blue shorts that reached barely a third of the way down from his waist to his thighs, white socks with blue-and-gold trim that reached almost to the bottom of his knees, and white Converse "Chuck Taylor" sneakers.

He looked as if he had emerged from the cover of a Boys' Life magazine. His brown hair was cut short, and looked as if it was form-fitted to his head. He had been sweating, but his hair seemed to be almost immune from moisture. He had a rugged chin and a small nose, and his face seemed to dare any whiskers to emerge from it. In short, he looked incapable of appearing ruffled, even if he had just played basketball for five hours – which, in fact, he just had.

"Hey man, how you doing?" Chris said as he extended his right hand, and the two exchanged a seventies-style handshake – with their thumbs interlocked, their other four fingers wrapped around each other's hand, as if they were about to arm-wrestle, only without a table on which to rest their elbows.

Chris recognized Matt Murdoch, with whom he had attended high school since ninth grade. At about five-foot-nine, with average hands and a build that seemed average, at best, Murdoch didn't cut the figure of an exceptional athlete.

But Chris had played basketball with and against him, and had seen him play at various levels, and he knew that if Matt Murdoch was nothing else, on a basketball court, he *was* exceptional.

"What you doing?" Chris said. "Hanging around waiting for UCLA to call?"

"Naw," Murdoch said, his unchanged expression indicating that he probably wouldn't have been surprised if he *had* gotten a call from

California at that moment. "I was just playing ball with some of those guys from St. Paul's. You know … those guys … they practically live out here."

"You show them some moves?"

"I held my own," Murdoch said with a laugh. He had, in fact, put on a show for the St. Paul's boys, making all but one or two of his shots, and blowing past each one who even attempted to cover him. He dished off at least three or four behind-the-back passes around startled opponents, to even-more-startled teammates. It got to a point where all he had to do, through at least a half-dozen games, was make one dribble, take one step, and the other guys on the court basically stopped doing anything and just watched him.

Chris had seen it plenty of times, from both ends. He was taller than Murdoch, but in his wildest dreams, he could not conjure up having anything resembling his on-court speed, his array of moves, and his seemingly metaphysical on-court sense. He knew the day would come when he would tell people, "Murdoch … oh yeah, I know him. Played with him dozens of times!"

"So, what you been up to this summer?" Murdoch said.

"Not much," Chris replied. "Working. In fact, I'm on my way there now."

"Where to?

"Blake."

"Blake?"

"Yeah … Blake! You know, the Blake Silk Mill …"

As soon as he said it, something in his subconscious sparked, and he quickly, as per the tester's admonition, corrected himself.

"Actually," he said. "Blake *Tex-tiles*!"

Murdoch shrugged. He already had college recruiters calling him and banging on his door. If he wanted a summer job, somebody would find it for him, and it almost certainly would involve him holding a basketball most of the time, at a summer camp or someplace. He surely would not be anywhere near the inside of a factory.

"Sounds like fun," he said sarcastically.

"Well, there's not much to it," Chris said. "But at least I can go buy a couple of albums or go to the pizza place if I want, you know? What sucks though is that it's a split shift."

"What's that mean?"

"Well, you work one week of days and then one week of nights," Chris said. "You go in at six in the morning until two in the afternoon one week, and then the next week, you're in two in the afternoon til ten at night."

Murdoch gave that a Bronx cheer. "Pffft!"

"Yeah, that's where I'm going now, to start at two," Chris said. "And there's a floorlady there who makes everybody miserable. But hey, I'm not gonna be doing it much longer. In fact, I'm going to tell them tonight that I'm leaving in two weeks."

"Cool," Murdoch said, although he wasn't sure what a floorlady was. "Why? You gonna do football again? That starts up in two weeks, don't it?"

"Well, I'm gonna try," Chris said. "Just had my physical yesterday. We'll see how it goes. I'll give it a shot. If I can just make the kickoff team or something, I'll be happy. They have a lot of ends, you know. Might switch to tackle."

Murdoch looked him up and down. "You big enough to play tackle?"

"No," he said. "But I know all the plays from playing next to them the last couple of years. They always need guys to play there. You know, everybody wants to be a split end."

Murdoch nodded. Chris figured that if Murdoch ever went out for football, they'd probably make him a split end, and he'd catch twenty touchdown passes and have even more cheerleaders drooling over him than he did already. But he also knew that the basketball coach would likely form a posse to snatch Murdoch from practice if he even went near the football field.

"You know, Matt, sometimes I wish I went to St. Paul's," Chris said.

"Why's that?" Murdoch said. "Don't tell me you don't like girls!"

"No!" Chris said. "It just would be nice to go out for football without having a hundred other guys trying out too."

"Yeah," Murdoch said, laughing. "We have enough guys to field teams for three schools. St. Pauls … they're lucky if they get thirty guys out. Then again, they get about a hundred out for basketball, so I guess it all works out, eh?"

"Like you'd have to worry," Chris said, poking him in the chest. "Mister All-County hoopster. Couple more years, and you'll be playing in the NBA."

"Yeah right," he said. "I just hope I make the team this year."

"Oh yeah, sure," Chris said. "They're gonna cut a two-time all-star who scored thirty in a district playoff game … when he was a freshman! You're so full of …"

Murdoch smiled a confident smile. He had the whole routine down pat. He knew he was good, and he knew that he had already punched his ticket to at least playing high-level college basketball. As long as he didn't fuck up – didn't get some dumb chick pregnant, or didn't get caught driving drunk – he was set. In fact, Chris doubted that anything would happen to Murdoch even if he did any of those things. The kid had it made.

"Well, anyway, I gotta run," Murdoch said. "See you in school in a few weeks. And good luck breaking the news to your bosses up there. I'm sure they're just gonna beg you to stay!"

"Well, one or two might," Chris said.

"You gonna stick it to that lady before you go?"

"Maggie? Hmmm! Don't give me any ideas!"

At that, Chris and Murdoch did what later would be known as a low five, and each went his own way. Chris knew Murdoch really didn't have to run; he pretty much made his own schedule. Basketball games, jobs, chicks, cars … they'd all wait *for him.*

But a skinny bobbin boy contemplating a senior-year shift to tackle didn't have that luxury. If he didn't shake his ass, he'd spend his first few minutes at the Blake listening to a dried-up floorlady rip him a new one for getting there four minutes past two o'clock, instead of at two on the dot.

21: BREAKING AND RUNNING

A sweaty, hard-breathing bobbin boy clocked in at two o'clock, having run up the hill and up the stairs in order to make it to the time clock on time. He wanted to run into the men's room and wash up, but he knew that would result in Maggie following him out of the room toward his work station, and that she would would turn a thirty-second wash-up into a federal case.

"It's after two o'clock!" she would bellow as she tailed him out of the room. "You're supposed to be at your station at two."

Upon telling her that he wanted to wash up first, she would corner him near the big bobbins and relentlessly badger him about how he should have gotten there a few minutes early if he wanted to do that. She had to be the only woman he ever met who would criticize a kid for washing his hands!

So he never did it. He just went to his station and, luckily, she hadn't noticed that he wasn't there promptly at two. She did rush by around three minutes after the hour, and while he was still sweaty and breathing hard, at least he was there, and all she did was grimace as she scurried by.

They were into their third calendar month of this game, and Maggie had not given Chris the slightest indication that she either respected him or his work ethic. She still seemed to hold him in contempt; granted, she treated just about everybody the same way, or worse. Still, Chris wondered why she seemed unwilling to at least concede that, for a sixteen-year-old working at his first job, he wasn't doing too badly. Couldn't she at least say thanks just once after he made his rounds, or something?

Then again, that sort of positive reinforcement didn't seem to be in the DNA of anybody in management at Blake Textiles. George, for instance, seemed to think he was paying you a compliment if he just ignored you. He couldn't imagine George actually patting a worker on the back.

Occasionally, Tony would give Chris a nod if he did something that Tony told him to do. It wasn't as much a nod, though, as a quick vertical jerk of the head.

Then again, wasn't that whole generation like that? His father wasn't much better. Neither were any males of his father's generation. They seemed to abhor anything resembling positive reinforcement. It was as if congratulating a sixteen-year-old for doing some menial task would be a sign of weakness, would constitute a lacking of manhood.

"Nobody told me I was doing a good job when I was chopping trees at the CCC camp!" he could hear them bark. *"Pat on the back? What that kid needs is a good kick in the ass!"*

That was the mindset. And Chris was well aware of it as he pondered how to tell Tony, the only foreman for whom he had ever worked, that he was going to be leaving his job in two weeks so that he could take one last shot at becoming a varsity football player.

Chris Tiller was not necessarily a bad football player. He had never gotten any formal training – nobody sent their sons to sports camps in those days, and his mother wouldn't let him play midget football.

He struggled through a nondescript season as a freshman end in 1968, the first year his school even fielded a freshman team. He spent most of his time standing on the sidelines – the coach wouldn't let anybody sit on the bench. He got in a few games in the final two minutes, and his biggest accomplishment came in one game when he was wide open in the end zone, with not a defender within twenty feet of him, and the quarterback lofted the ball so far over his head that all he didn't even try to jump for it. He stood there and watched his best chance at a touchdown sail a dozen yards past the back of the end zone.

He did nothing to prepare for his sophomore year, and quit the team after one week of practice. He'd been intimidated and beaten physically, and it should have been the end of his football career. But somehow, during the summer of 1970, with his annual trip to the shore out of the picture, he got himself into pretty decent shape, running a mile or so a couple of times a week, and basically putting himself into the proper mindset for a return to football.

And he stuck it out. He ended up a junior varsity backup, but he lasted the season, and got to go to the post-season banquet, and even got a trophy to show for it. Classmates who didn't even know he played football were shocked to see him on the stage for the season's final pep rally, and over the winter and during the spring, he actually looked forward to going back out for the team in the fall of 1971. As a senior, he knew he more or less had to be put on the varsity squad – at least for the home games.

He figured that if he could show some grit during the summer practices, he might get a shot to try to block punts or something.

And as he told Murdoch, he was even willing to switch to tackle!

To do all that, though, he had to start practice in two weeks. He worried that he wasn't in shape for that, but he figured that the eight hours of work he'd been putting in daily couldn't hurt. Plus, he'd been walking either to or from the mill every day all summer.

First, though, he had to tell Tony that he was leaving the mill. He got his chance when Tony strolled past his station about an hour before lunch.

"Hey … uh … Tony?" he said.

"Yeah, Tiller," Tony said. "What you want?"

"I wanted to tell you something."

"Huh?" said Tony, straining to hear him above the din of the machinery.

"I wanted to tell you something!" he said.

"Well, let's go back there," Tony said, pointing to the area where Shirley worked during the day. They walked back, and the noise abated slightly.

"Well ... um ... Tony ... I ... uh ..." Chris stammered. He had never had to do anything like this before, and he wasn't sure what to say. He still felt slightly uncomfortable calling adults such as Tony by their first names, and now he had to tell the guy he was leaving.

"Jesus, Tiller, what the hell is on your mind? You want a raise or something?"

"No, actually, I wanted to ... I wanted to tell you I'm gonna be leaving in two weeks."

Tony looked at him, his eyebrows arching. He almost seemed puzzled, as if the thought of Chris leaving had never occurred to him.

"Leaving?" he said. "You mean you're quitting?"

"Well ... yeah," Chris said. "I mean, this only was a summer job."

Tony rubbed his chin.

"Hmm," he said. "Well, I thought ... I mean, I was under the impression, anyway ... I mean ... based on my conversations with George ... I was led to believe you were going to be working here after school."

Chris leaned back, surprised. George and Tony had been talking about him? They actually had spent management time discussing his situation? The big guys, talking about a bobbin boy?

"Well, I never even ... Nobody ever asked me about that," he said.

"Wasn't it on your work papers?"

"Wasn't what on my work papers?"

"When we signed your work papers, I guess we put down that you were going to work during the summer, and then twenty hours a week beginning in September. That's pretty standard procedure around here for high school kids."

"I never noticed," Chris said. "But I really just came here for the summer."

Tony looked him over, as if he was trying to formulate a counter-proposal that might keep him on past Labor Day.

"You got something planned?" he said.

"Well … school!" Chris said. "And football practice starts in two weeks."

Tony, who had played high school football himself in the pre-face mask era, looked at the gangly teen before him. He didn't say it, but his expression made it pretty clear that he found the notion of this kid being a football player somewhat comical.

"*You* play football?" he said.

"Well, yeah!" Chris said. "I played last year. I mean, I didn't play much, or even dress with the varsity … well, I did for two home games. But I'm a senior this year, and they have to let me do something!"

"I suppose, but … jeez … if you ain't gonna play much …"

"Well, I'm hoping to play a little bit!" Chris said. "We're gonna have a pretty good team this year."

Tony kept looking him over. He was trying to comprehend why a kid who knew he wasn't going to play much would leave a paying job for the prospect of being a benchwarmer on a football team. In his day, Tony played guard on offense, tackle on defense, was in on every punt, kickoff, and extra point. He couldn't imagine why a kid would want to be on a team if he wasn't going to play.

But there was more to it than that. *This kid had a job already!* In Tony's day, *that* was the brass ring; even if you were an All-County ballplayer, you dropped everything if you had a job lined up. Nobody thought much about playing college ball or anything like that. The whole idea was to get a job, usually once you graduated from high school. If you had a job lined up while you were still in school, especially a steady job at a place like the Blake, you were a golden boy! You might even be set for life!

But here was a kid passing on a job in order to … maybe play on the kickoff team? Where did these kids nowadays get ideas like this?

"Anyway," Chris said. "My dad said to give you two weeks' notice. So I guess I'll work this week, and then days next week."

Tony began to rub the bridge of his nose with his right hand. He knew that losing Chris meant he would have to send one of the fellows from Frank's crew over to work on the big bobbins, at least temporarily. That usually did not work out very well.

"Well, let me tell you what George was thinking," he said. "We figured you'd work four to eight, Monday through Friday nights, after school. You'd switch between me and Ray's groups. That way, we'd have a big bobbin boy here every night. You know, we've really been counting on you since you came over here."

For a moment, Chris pondered the sheer joy of spending every other week with Molly as his floorlady instead of Maggie. It was tempting to think of being able to walk out of work on a Friday night, knowing he wouldn't have to see Maggie for another ten days.

"So four hours every night, and different foremen and floorladies every week, huh?" he said.

Tony smiled. "I know what you're thinking!"

Chris also thought briefly about what he could do with the money he could get from working twenty hours a week on a permanent basis. A better stereo, especially with some big-ass speakers! A new TV, to replace the hand-me-down set in his room, which, on a good night, picked up maybe two channels. And … down the road … maybe … a … *a car*!

It was tempting. Especially when he glanced over toward where the girl in the bandana worked. He tried to imagine seeing her around Christmas time, when, he fantasized, she'd be dressed a lot differently than she was during the summer.

And … if he stayed … there was a chance he might get to talk to her! He must have drifted into a semi-conscious state just thinking about it, because next thing he knew, Tony was poking him in the chest.

"Tiller!" he said. "I asked you if you're sure about this!"

"Oh ... oh ... yeah!" he said. "I ... I think I'd be really ticked off at myself if we won the championship or something, and I wasn't on the team at least."

Tony shrugged. "All right then," he said. "I'll let Maggie know."

"I'm sure she'll be thrilled," Chris said.

"Well, maybe I'll hold off, then," Tony said. "Maybe you'll have a change of heart. But I do have to tell George, though."

Chris nodded and looked at Tony. It dawned on him that once he walked out of the mill, he'd probably never see the guy again. He hadn't thought about that before. But Tony would probably retire, and then die, and maybe, if Chris happened to be looking at the obituary page that morning, he would read about it in the newspaper. Is this how it always went in the working world? Did you just walk away from people like this, never to see them again?

"I ... I guess I'm sorry, Tony," he said.

"Aww, don't worry about it," Tony said. "People leave here all the time. Most of the time, we don't worry about the door hitting them in the ass on the way out. But you ... you did a good job for a new kid. This was your first job, wasn't it?"

"Yeah," he said. "I guess I'll never be able to say that again, right?"

Tony poked him in the chest again. Then he turned and walked away, rubbing the back of his head with his right hand as he strolled back toward the foreman's station, no doubt pondering personnel moves as he walked.

He'd figure something out, of course. The town was filled with potential bobbin boys. One of them would wander in and take Chris Tiller's place, and Tony and Maggie and George would no doubt give little thought to the one who ran the big bobbin station on one split shift for one summer in the early seventies.

On the other hand, Chris was sweating as he went back to work, and not from physical exertion. His body was making it clear to him that he had just passed one of the many mile markers in his life, and when you're sixteen, it's hard to fathom that you have just done something for the first, and only time.

But this one was in the books: Chris Tiller would never give his first two weeks' notice to his first foreman on his first job again.

22: SERENADE FOR THE NIGHT SHIFT

Chris worked nights the rest of the week, as word began to spread that he was leaving. Tony did tell Maggie and George, but neither one of them said anything to Chris; in fact, he hadn't seen George all week.

Around eight o'clock on Friday night, he put down the tools of his soon-to-end trade and headed to the men's room. This would be the final break of his nightside career at The Blake, and while he would have breaks during the day on his final week, he sensed there was something almost benedictory about this one.

From his first night at the mill, Chris had noticed that the eight o'clock break was something special. And after a week or so, he realized that one worker in particular seemed to hold court during the eight o'clock break.

He'd been quiet when Chris first noticed him on his first-ever four o'clock break, but it didn't take long for Chris to realize that Richie usually was in his element during the last break of the night shift.

Richie only worked nights, so Chris only saw him every other week. Since that afternoon when he'd first seen Richie in the men's room, he learned that Richie had, in fact, had polio when he was young, and that his bizarre walk and strange mannerisms were due, in part, to the devastating effects of the illness.

He was, by job title and by his duties, a stock boy. He was probably in his late twenties, but he looked somewhat more ... eccentric ... than anybody else of that generation whom Chris had ever met. He had a haircut like the kid in the "Dutch Boy" paint ads, but Chris thought it might have been a wig. He really was a creepy figure. His hands and arms never seemed to work in unison. He usually dragged at least one foot when he walked. He had numerous facial tics, including a habit of jerking his head back violently on occasion, which remained as startling to Chris as it had been the first time he saw it.

No matter how hot it was outside, Richie always wore a long-sleeved shirt, usually a white or light blue one. His pants were always double-knit, usually dark brown, but sometimes maroon. He always wore not work shoes, but dressy brown boots that rose to just above the ankle, with a zipper on one side.

He rarely spoke whenever Claude was around. But otherwise, he talked all the time, and when he was holding court during the last break of the night shift, his voice seemed to hang in the air of the men's room, as if the darkening air outside lifted it up and kept it there.

He had a speech impediment, and he tended to spray out many of his words, so nobody ever stood face-to-face with him. He rarely finished a sentence without blinking rapidly, and he always had a cigarette, which he either puffed as if he was drawing a seminal breath, or which he held out daintily, in a manner Chris – who had been surrounded by male smokers seemingly since birth – had never seen before.

One other thing about Richie: He seemed to talk about almost nothing else but drinking, getting drunk, and about bars and bartenders. If he spent a combined two minutes that summer talking about baseball, or music, or the weather, or politics, Chris couldn't remember it.

Chris could have had an indefinite number of opportunities to hear Richie talk, if only he had elected to stay on and work at the mill after school. But because he was leaving, and because word had spread that he was, this was to be his final break of his final night shift, the final time he would listen to this strange concoction of a human being called Richie.

"... so I told this bartender ... I said ... 'Make me a gin and tonic ... and go light on the tonic!'" he said, before noticing that Chris had entered the men's room.

As often happened, Richie followed that line with a cackling laugh, a self-absorbing guffaw that attempted to validate the joke, while the two or three other guys in the room just smiled.

"And here comes my co-worker!" he said, pointing the hand holding his cigarette at Chris. "Ending one of his last night shifts. Or should I say ... one of his last night *shits*!"

Again, Richie cackled.

"Very funny, Richie, very funny." Chris said. "But I do still have a week of days to work next week."

"And that gives you another week with dear old Maggie!"

Jeff, who often tried to goad Richie along various paths of conversation, looked up at him. "Hey Richie," he said. "How come you never tried to ... you know ... get it on with Maggie?"

Richie frowned, and this time he pointed his cigarette hand directly down at the little hippie bobbin boy. "Shut your God-damned mouth, boy!" he said, practically screaming. "You think my pecker's made outta lead or somethin?"

This time, everybody except Richie laughed. He took a big drag from his cigarette, jerked his head back, and then twisted his face into an expression somewhere between contentment and misery.

"Anyways, I am gonna get outta this fuckin' place in two hours," he spat. "I'm gonna go to the Sable Room and tell those bartenders there to make me the biggest God-damned scotch-and-water they ever saw!"

"They'll tell you to fuck off!" Jeff said.

"*No they won't!*" Richie responded, his eyes seeming to narrow as he glared down at Jeff. "No they won't! I know shit about those cock suckers that they don't want anybody else to know! They won't screw around with me!"

Jeff continued to prod him. He was so adept at pushing Richie's buttons that it was like watching some sort of shrimpy Wizard of Oz behind a curtain.

"I thought you hung out at the Club Athens," Jeff said, referring to a particularly sleazy bar downtown that some people claimed was a gay bar.

"Now stop that!" Richie spewed. "I don't hang out at no Club Athens!"

"So you're saying you ain't never been there?" Jeff said.

Richie had a choice: He could continue to claim he'd never been to the Club Athens, or he could tell what he considered a funny story.

He chose the latter.

"I'll tell you what," he said, pointing at Jeff. "That bartender there really pissed me off the other night …"

As if on cue, Chris flushed the urinal he was using. Richie and Jeff both looked at him, the former scowling and the latter giggling.

"… he really pissed me off!" Richie continued. "He accused me of walking out without paying for my drink! Would I do something like that?"

"Well, you don't make that much money here," said Chris, refreshed and ready to join this odd conversation. "And you have that big sports car …"

"I don't drive no sports car!" Richie sputtered. He was hovering between amused and agitated, but he was used to it. "Shit, I drive a sixty-five Buick … you know that. And anyway … my ball joints are all fucked up …"

They all giggled. Even Richie thought it was amusing.

"I got fucked-up ball joints!" he said.

"Well," countered Jeff, "at least you ain't got fucked-up …"

"*Never mind!*" Richie roared, cutting him off. He took another long drag of his cigarette — Chris wondered how he took such long drags and didn't have to light new ones every two minutes — and seemed to make a serious face as he looked at Chris.

"But listen, I don't hang out at the Club Athens," he said. "Okay?"

"It doesn't matter to me … I'm too young to get in anyway," Chris said.

"And you better not try!" Richie said. "I better not see you in there!"

Chris shook his head as the door opened and Brian walked in. The young machine operator had small bandages on about half of his fingertips.

"Here comes a real working man!" Richie said.

Brian went over to one of the urinals, where he obviously didn't have an easy time using his hands. After about fifteen seconds, he flushed, and came back over to sit down near Jeff.

"Yep, a real worker!" Richie said.

"I guess so," Brian said.

Richie was intrigued by the bandages on Brian's fingers. It was fairly obvious he had hurt himself on one of the machines, but Richie wasn't going to let him out of the men's room without having the opportunity to comment on it.

"So what happened to your hands?" he said bluntly. "Looks bad."

"Aw, I got careless and got my hands stuck in the machine," Brian said. "It was scary. I couldn't stop it and my hands could've gotten caught in there a lot worse. One of the guys had to come over and stop it, and I guess I'm lucky I only got my fingertips pinched a little. They'll be all right in a day or two."

"You shoulda gone home," Richie said.

"Yeah, and Russell had a good laugh about it. But I guess I'm lucky Maggie didn't hit me on the head when I had to stop the machine. I guess she'd rather see you get killed, or at least lose an arm, than slow things down."

Richie paused, as if he was trying to think of something really funny to say. After a few seconds, his eyes widened, and he got that expression that a fellow gets when he can't wait to tell a great joke he'd just heard.

"Well, I'll tell ya one thing," he said. "You sure ain't gonna be able to finger your wife's pussy for a while!"

Jeff bowed his head and put it in his hands. Chris just shook his head. Brian seemed shocked. But Richie acted as if he'd just hit a home run in the World Series.

"Yeah, you better call home!" he said, cackling away. "Tell your wife you won't be fingering her pussy tonight!"

Nobody was laughing. Richie couldn't figure it out. Did they all know something he didn't know?

"Hey, don't tell me you ain't married!" he said.

"Well, yes," said Brian. "Yes I am."

And then he paused, and to Chris and Jeff and the other guy in the room, it was as if they could see Richie about to have a freight train run up his backside, and they couldn't do anything about it.

"Yes, I'm married," Brian said. "But I'm also studying to be a minister."

Jeff put his right thumb and index finger to the bridge of his nose and rubbed it as if he had the world's worst sinus headache. The other two shook their heads. But Richie, after a few seconds of appearing surprised, got that confident look again. He took an almost delicate puff of his cigarette, and he looked at Brian.

"Well," he said. "At least you're not studying to be a Catholic priest!"

Eyes rolled, and Chris could feel himself groan.

"Shut the fuck up, Richie!" yelled Jeff.

Richie appeared taken aback, and he took his left hand and waved off Jeff's criticism.

"No, wait!" he said. "The guy said he's studying to be a minister, right? Not a priest? A minister!"

Richie paused, and it was obvious he thought he'd come up with yet another profound thought.

"And let's face it," he said. "Ministers *do* fuck their wives!"

Jeff's head fell back so hard it hit the wall with a thud. Brian shook his head, but giggled. Chris bit his lower lip, unable to think of anything else to do.

"Richie," said Brian, who seemed stuck somewhere between offended and amused. "You are something else!"

Shaking his head, the bandaged Brian walked out of the men's room, no doubt fully aware of the totally accurate statement Richie had made, but also shocked that somebody had the temerity to actually say it to him – in a textile mill men's room, at night, no less!

"Oh well," Chris said. "Nothing else to do tonight except go home and watch Johnny Carson, I guess."

"Oh well," Richie said. "I guess it's time to go back to work … then it will be time to get the fuck out of here and go get drunk."

Then the door swung open again. It was Claude, dressed in his usual flashy attire, except that he had on a dark summer jacket, the result of him having been working outside for about an hour. As soon as Claude entered the room, Richie vacated the window position he had been occupying.

"Now listen up, all you guys workin' nights!" Claude roared. "I want you to do your own jobs the rest of the night … cause I gotta get outta here on time tonight."

"Got a date, Claude?" Jeff said.

"Man, you gotta ask?" Claude said. "I got a date. And I can't be late! And you know that when I come in here every day, I do my job, like takin' all that junk outside to the dumpster, like I been doin' for the last hour. And normally I do everybody else's job … but I ain't doin' everybody else's job tonight, 'cause I gotta get outta here at ten! So all you guys … you do your jobs, 'cause I can't do your jobs for y'all tonight!"

Claude lit up a cigarette and took the spot Richie had occupied. Richie's face turned stern, as if he knew his role had changed with Claude's arrival.

Once in the spot, Claude began his song again:

"I do my job, and then when I'm done with my job, I do everybody else's job. I do Frank's job and Richie's job and …"

Claude paused and looked at Chris, who was getting ready to leave. Chris looked at Claude, straight in the eyes. Then, after a few seconds that seemed to take forever, Claude smiled, his gold tooth flashing, and then his big left eye closed and then opened again, as he gave the teenaged bobbin boy a wink for which he'd been waiting all summer.

"… and then I do Chris's job!"

It really was a simple thing, and Chris never would really find out if Claude had actually known his name all along. But he'd sure never called him by his name before. So, no vote of confidence from an employer, no positive job review, no raise, or no other honor, would ever mean as much to Chris Tiller on any job as did that simple line during Claude's song on the last break of his last night shift of his first summer job.

Chris looked at the evening sky out the men's room window for the last time, then turned and walked toward the door. Behind him, ushering him out, was Claude's now-treasured new lyric, sung in that falsetto voice to which Chris had become so accustomed since he first heard it in that grimy old men's room at the mill:

"… and I do Chris's job … and I do Chris's job … and I do … Chris's … job!!!"

23: WIN ONE FOR THE TESTER

The second week of August was the last week of Chris Tiller's summer at Blake Textiles. He spent it working the day shift, and for the first four days of the week, things were pretty much as they had been all summer.

He helped the tester almost every day, and he chatted with Shirley as much as her workload permitted. He didn't see much of Claude, who was also working days that week, and he chatted with others, such as Andy and Carol, as circumstances permitted.

He didn't talk much to Tony, had no contact with George, and tried to avoid Maggie. He wasn't certain that she knew he was leaving, as she had said nothing to him about it. Prior to Friday, the longest conversation he had with anybody about his leaving was with Will.

The two of them usually chatted in the morning, either before the start of the shift, or on occasion during the first break. But most of their conversations were just small talk.

But on Thursday morning, Will was having his usual coffee when he brought up the subject of Chris's departure.

"So, I hear you're about to jump ship, there, eh buddy?" he said.

"Um … yeah," said Chris. "Football practice starts next week."

"Hey, gotta have priorities, right?" said Will.

Chris looked at Will, who had a noticeable pot belly, and whose butt wasn't that small either. Then he looked down at his own belly, which for whatever reason, had grown a bit during the summer, despite all the pushing carts, and the walking to and from work.

"I don't know about this, though," Chris said, tapping his midsection, which had a long way to go before it approached anything near what Will was carrying around. "I had a little one last year, but I lost it by the time school started."

"You'll lose it, you'll lose it," Will said, laughing. "Betcha it'll be gone within a week."

"Hope so," Chris said.

"Hey," said Will, laughing and tapping his own belly. "I wish we all had someplace to go to lose it, ya know?"

And that was pretty much the extent of it until Friday morning. Shirley came in around eight o'clock, and when Chris got back from his first break, she greeted him with her typical smile.

"Good morning Chris!" she said. "Big day for you, eh?"

"Yeah, it's been busy ..."

"You *know* that's not what I mean!" she said. "Don't try to be coy with me kid!"

He smiled as she tapped him on the arm.

"You're leaving us after today, in case you forgot!" she said.

Chris laughed some more. He lost count of the times he tried to work out in his mind how the same textile mill could employ one woman as nice as Shirley, and at the same time enable such a miserable woman as Maggie.

"I really don't know how many people know," he said. "I told Tony, but I really didn't talk to too many others about it. Will asked me about it yesterday. I don't know who else might know."

"Are you kidding?" she said, looking over her glasses at him as she grabbed some samples to begin her work. "You're in the gossip capital of the state here, sweetie! Gosh, for the last day or two, that's just about all I've been hearing … 'Chris this,' or 'that big bobbin boy that.'"

"Really?"

"Oh yeah!" she said. Then she looked over toward the area where Chris had begun to look, toward the girl in the bandana.

"I guarantee you … she doesn't know," he said, sighing.

He was still looking over toward her when he heard someone approaching. He looked and saw the tester walking toward him.

"Well, well, well," he said. "It's Mister Short-Timer!"

"Huh?" said Chris, who had never heard that term before.

"Short-timer!" the tester said. "Wait `til you get in the Army someday, then you'll know what it means."

"Oh … okay!" Chris said, still not getting it.

"So, were you gonna leave today without coming upstairs to say goodbye?"

"Oh no!" Chris said. "I was gonna come up after lunch. I figured we could come up with some reason you needed me up there, in case you-know-who went looking for me."

"Well, what if I wasn't there?"

"I don't know, I guess I'd have waited!"

They both laughed. Chris really dreaded saying goodbye to certain people, and of course, the tester was on top of that list.

"So, you goin' out for football then?" the tester said. Chris was beginning to wonder if there was something in the morning paper about his leaving, given how much everybody seemed to know about it.

"That's the plan," he said. "I would have worked at least until school started, but I wanna be there for the start of practice next week."

The tester looked him over, much as Tony had. Chris prepared for another round of "You *really* play football?" from the tester, but as usual, the tester confounded him by asking him about his position.

"So, what position you play?" he said.

"Well, I was an end last year," Chris said. "Mostly J.V."

The tester smiled and then pulled his head back and stared at the ceiling. It was as if he was trying to conjure up something special to say, and once he did, it seemed to Chris as if he was delivering a lecture to a large audience, not to one kid in a noisy textile mill.

"You know, I've always been amazed by the tight end," he said. He began to move his hands around, simulating the motion of a tight end catching a football. "As far as I'm concerned, the tight end is the most amazing player in football."

Chris looked at him curiously. At his school, they didn't even *have* a tight end. They were still playing seven-man front football, with two tight ends, so to speak.

But the tester seemed to be in an almost evangelical mood. As the machinery hummed around them, and as bobbins piled up around the floor, he continued his lecture.

"You know, sometimes, the tight end has to do nothing but block," said the tester, who then got down in a three-point stance and softly rose up to demonstrate an almost perfect blocking technique on his startled young subject.

"But sometimes, they have to be great receivers," he said. At that, he stood up, took a few steps, and simulated catching a pass over his right shoulder.

"And you know, it's always the tight end who has to make the tough catch," he said. "He's the guy they throw to when it's real crowded in the end zone, or when they need a first down. He ends up getting hit by those linebackers."

And then, the tester bumped into Chris, bounced off him as if he was Larry Csonka breaking a tackle, and darted around one or two stacks of racks of soiled wooden bobbins.

"And you have to be good on defense, too," he said, walking back toward Chris. "Let's say you go out for a pass, and the quarterback throws a bad one ..."

The next thing Chris knew, the tester was in Johnny Unitas mode, his left arm extended in front of him, and his right arm simulating the throwing of a pass.

"And it gets intercepted," he said, at which he emerged from quarterback mode and took on the stance of a defensive player. Chris wondered if he wasn't going to get tackled to the wooden floor.

"Well then, the tight end has to stop playing offense, and he has to switch right to defense," the tester said. "They have to know how to tackle. Then again, most of 'em play defensive end, too. And that's not an easy position!"

Chris braced himself for a demonstration of a defensive end sacking the quarterback, but then the tester settled down. He was sweating and breathing hard.

"Wow, you sure you don't wanna try out for some team yourself?" Chris said. "Looks like you could play a lot of positions there!"

The tester smiled, took a deep breath, and put his hand on Chris's left shoulder. Chris looked around, worried that Maggie might have seen some or all of it, and would be storming toward them for a confrontation.

"Look here!" the tester said. "Don't you worry about Maggie or any of those people right now! You get the hell outta here at two o'clock and don't look back. Don't spend the next couple of hours worrying about what a couple of people who make up for their own inadequacies by bullying a bunch of teenagers and dimwits around … don't worry about what any of them think!"

Chris smiled.

"So listen, I'll be looking for you when you play Woodlawn," the tester said, referring to the high school in the town where the tester lived, his alma mater, a school that traditionally had one of the area's most powerful teams. "They have a pretty good team this year."

"That's our first game, actually," Chris said.

"Great!"

"But don't expect me to be playing much," Chris said. "I'll be lucky to get on the kickoff team."

The tester breathed hard through his nose. He stared at Chris, the look reminiscent of one a father would give to a son of whom he expected a lot, but in whom he had even more pride.

"Hey, you never know," he said. "Look at me. I was just a worker, and then the chemist showed me the ropes, and now George thinks twice before he starts with me. He knows it'd take a long time to train my replacement if I left. That's *if* they could train one."

Chris bit his lip. He'd heard it all before. But then he realized that after this day, he probably would never hear it again.

"Anyway," the tester said. "He knows I can go to DuPont if I have to!"

And at that, the tester laughed loudly, so loudly that it seemed to burst, like a tornado, above the noise of the machinery. He was still chuckling as he walked away, without another word, toward the freight elevator and back to his domain at the top of The Blake.

24: BEGINNING THE END

Chris didn't sleep much, if at all, on Thursday night going into Friday. Even for a sixteen-year-old, a six o'clock start requires some rest, but Chris had been an adrenaline machine all week, and the anticipation of his final day at The Blake had him wound up.

For the most part, he couldn't wait to leave. If the experience taught him anything, it was that the factory life wasn't for him. It was fine for a summer, but to have to do it week in and week out, with no end game, just weeks and months and years and decades flying by, that was not for him.

And of course, he couldn't wait to get away from certain people, especially Maggie.

But he knew he would miss the others, and he also knew he'd never see them again. He fervently hoped that the next summer would see him preparing for college, and that perhaps he would be able to get a summer job that didn't involve the factory life.

He couldn't envision a scenario in which he would even apply at the Blake again. He would see if he could get a job where his father worked, or with one of his siblings. He had satisfied his own sense of independence by getting his first job on his own, but there was no sense being silly about that.

His father dropped him off on Friday and there certainly was no fanfare associated with that. Much as he enjoyed seeing his son work at his first job, he was glad to be relieved of his chauffeuring duties.

So Chris clocked in as usual, said hello to Will, and chatted briefly with Shirley before going on break at eight o'clock. Of course, Will was in the men's room when he got there.

"Strange feeling, isn't it?" he said.

"Yeah, kind of counting the hours," Chris replied.

"Funny, but I've been here so long I forgot about all the times I left other jobs," Will said. "For cryin' out loud, I must have quit a dozen or so before I landed here."

Chris felt ambivalent about going any further into Will's background. On one hand, he genuinely liked the guy, and, in a strange way, admired his dexterity with the machinery of the mill. He wasn't sure how or when Will developed it, and he sure didn't see any particular use for it outside the walls of The Blake, but he still admired it, especially since there was no way he could even approach it.

But he couldn't help thinking there was something a bit odd about Will. Even back then, who, outside of a few Las Vegas performers, dressed like that? Was Will fighting some sort of losing battle against his true age, trying, with the gold chains and the white shoes, to stave off becoming another Tony, or George? Was Will dousing some unpleasant part of his past with Faberge cologne and faux gold chains?

Chris preferred, therefore, not to know anymore, to keep Will as a pleasant older brother-type or cousin-type, whose personal business was best left personal.

"Well, good luck then, buddy," Will said as he left the men's room and went back out to the floor. "Maybe see you down the road."

They shook hands, and Chris followed him out of the men's room. Will went back to his machine, where, later in the day, he and Chris would have one more encounter.

But at this point, there was a round of bobbins to collect. When Chris went back to his station to get his cart, he saw the tester waiting there, talking, of course, to Shirley.

"Hard to believe, isn't it?" he said when Chris approached. "Last day … at last."

"Don't get me crying," Shirley said.

Chris just chuckled, but then, without even thinking, he said something he wouldn't have dared say a few months before.

"Don't I get a going-away present?" he said, chuckling.

"What do you think this is, a law office or something," the tester asked. "Not sure we have time here … Shirl, I don't think we ever gave anybody a going-away party or anything, did we?"

Shirley shook her head.

"Yeah, Chris, I'm afraid you're just gonna have to ride into the sunset this time," the tester said. "But you never know."

Shirley and the tester exchanged looks, and the tester just walked away again, back to his fifth-floor headquarters. Shirley went back to her area, and Chris, not really sure what he'd just heard, went on his rounds.

He collected bobbins from all the regular daytime workers. Maggie was busy with some issue on one of the machines, and she hardly noticed him. Claude was there, but he was pushing a huge crate onto a pallet; the man could be a human forklift at times.

By the time Chris got done making his rounds and cleaning off some of the bobbins for collection by the mysterious Darrell, it was almost time for lunch.

Just as he was about to head outside, he realized that he hadn't seen the girl with the bandana yet.

25: LUNCH ON THE ROCK

For most of the second half of his summer at The Blake, Chris had been eating lunch not on the front steps, or in the lunchroom, or even in the parking lot.

Quite by coincidence, he had taken to eating lunch in the spot in the woods right beyond the parking lot. As Floyd had years before, he had found a sort of quiet place on that rock, away from the noise and even from any of his coworkers.

He'd been eating there a few weeks before he blurted out that fact to Floyd. The tester seemed surprised that his summer protégé had found that rock, just as he had, but otherwise, he didn't seem to care. So as far as Chris was concerned, it was nothing but a coincidence.

So, on his final day at the Blake, he headed out to the rock. He sat down and took a deep breath. It was hot and sunny outside, but in the shaded area where he was sitting, it was cool and shady.

At ten in the morning, the air was clear for an August day, the humidity just starting to build toward afternoon. Chris could see the end of his summer at the Blake in sight.

He turned his head to the right to reach for his sandwich, and he could hear the sound of leaves rustling nearby.

And she was there. Dressed just as she had been the first time he saw her. She smiled, and Chris started to shake. He wasn't sure what to do, but when she motioned to him to slide over, he made room on the rock for her to sit next to him.

They were two teenagers working in a mill on a summer day in the early 1970s. It was still morning. They were a good ten minutes into a thirty-minute lunch break, and even if Chris had nothing to lose, she did. So this was not going to be some sort of teenaged sexual initiation scene – for either one of them.

And that really didn't matter. Chris had barely ever sat this close to a girl before, and certainly not one like this. He was shaking, and she was shaking a bit, as well. He had to squirm, in fact, and put his legs together a bit, just to avoid having her seeing the effect she was having on him.

As was her pattern, she didn't say a word. And Chris, inexperienced as he was, couldn't say anything at first. He just kept smiling at her.

Finally, the words came to him.

"Hello, my name is Chris, and …"

Before he could say more, she put her index finger to his lips. She shook her head. If she didn't know his name already, it was already more than she wanted to know. Somehow, he surmised, she knew this was his last day at work, and for whatever reason, she had come out to join him.

Had the tester set it up? Or maybe Claude? Shirley? Or had the girl just heard about it through the gossip mill, and decided to follow him into the woods?

Whatever the reason, Chris only wanted to know her name. He couldn't imagine leaving the Blake without at least knowing that.

But every time he tried to speak, she pressed her finger to his lips and shook her head.

He never even heard her voice.

But as the end of their lunch break loomed, she put his lips to his. If she had ever kissed like that before, he had not. But he took to it naturally. It was not an intense, powerful, passionate kiss; neither one was really capable of that yet. But for two teenagers passing each other in the summer, it was an indication of something that could be, something unknown, yet wonderful.

After the kiss, she smiled, and brushing the hair on his forehead, she got up, kissed him on the forehead, and smiled. Their eyes met and then she turned and walked away, back into the mill. Chris felt as if his throat was closing; his hands were shaking, and his entire body felt sparks from the physical effects of what had happened.

He waited a few more minutes, leaving his lunch on the ground. He would never go into that patch in the woods again. He would never sit on that rock again. And of course, he would never see her again.

26: THE INEVITABLE CLASH

Chris felt his head and heart pounding as he re-entered the mill. He spent the next two hours in a daze. He didn't speak to anybody. He couldn't bring himself to make a bobbin run right away, Maggie be damned.

But, inevitably, he had to do it. He did not go into the men's room for the noon break; he went into a remote area near the rear of the mill, where there was a small storage department, leading to a small outside enclave. He went there and just leaned against the building, feeling his head pounding and his heart pounding, and thinking over every interaction of the past few months, thinking over every decision. Should he stay on after all, forget about football and everything else, and just work a few nights a week?

Or would that be just hanging on past his time? He was never meant to be at the mill long; he knew that. He came as a sixteen-year-old stranger and would leave the same way, not even a grain of sand in the relentless wave of the mill's existence. In many ways, he could not have been less relevant to the long history of The Blake.

And after all, hadn't the tester said it best? These mills, they were all dinosaurs anyway. By the time Chris got to be the age the tester and Will and Shirley were now, these mills would all be closed down. The lucky buildings would become flea markets or warehouses, homes to art galleries or children's theaters.

The unlucky ones would rot and become home to rats and other vermin. Eventually they'd be torn down, and nobody would ever know they had been there.

He'd seen it happen to other old factories in the town; this one might not escape that fate.

And yet, he had touched the lives of people there. And they had certainly touched his. He doubted many of them – or any of them – would remember him. But he knew he would never forget them.

So, he went back in. And the machines hummed with greater intensity, as the mill machine kicked into high gear. The roar from noon until around one o'clock that day seemed to him more powerful and louder than ever.

He watched the clock. With about thirty minutes to go, he decided to make one last run. He was nearly finished when he turned the last corner on the way to his station, with just a few minutes to go in this unplanned summertime drama.

Of course, Maggie was there. He thought about it later, the emotion in her eyes. Was it hate? Anger? Jealousy? Frustration? Was it personal? She could be nasty to everybody.

Did she just find it impossible not to get one final burst of whatever it was that tormented her out toward this relatively insignificant sixteen-year-old, who, in another time, might have gone on to become something along the lines of what that kid Floyd had become several years before.

"So, you think you can do things your own way just because you're about to leave," she snorted. "Well you're still on the clock boy, and until then, you're mine!"

The roaring of the machines seemed to dim, and the pounding in his head seemed to intensify. He almost felt as if not only Will and Shirley and all the lesser bobbin boys, but also Claude and Richie and maybe everybody else who'd ever worked in the damned place, he felt as if they were all waiting to see what his final move would be.

His pounding brain, and the stress being triggered throughout his young body told him now was the time, the time to do what he said he would do, what he had waited all summer to do, what the tester somehow seemed to know he would someday do.

It was time to tell this shrill woman what she could do to herself, perhaps in a voice that would roar over the machinery, and would rest in the rafters of the Blake Silk Mill, or Textile Mill, or whatever, for as long as it stood, as a sort of monument, something to say that Chris Tiller had, in fact, been there.

But as the second hand moved on the clock on the wall, and as he waited for the notice that the shift was over, he thought of those times when the tester had so deftly handled her, and how nothing cut Maggie more deeply than the knowledge that she had not gotten the best of him.

So, as the two o'clock buzzer sounded the end of his summer at the Blake, Chris Tiller turned to the little bitch, glared at her, and said, in as polite a voice as even a sixteen-year-old angel could muster:

"Margaret ... Have a nice life!"

27: FAREWELL FROM A FRIEND

There was one final chore. Chris walked to the time clock, getting in line behind a few others and waiting to punch out. Perhaps if he had screamed at the top of his lungs for Maggie to go fuck herself, he would have been given a standing ovation by those clocking out. But nobody had heard him, it seemed, except for Maggie.

Still, word spreads quickly, even among the thunder of the mill. Once he clocked out and put his card into the week-ending box, he turned to leave for the final time. There, flanking the doorway, were Claude on the left, and the tester on the right.

"My man!" said Claude, slapping him five robustly as he approached, then putting him in a bear hug that somehow didn't break a few of the teen's ribs.

"I'm gonna have to do some extra work with you not here, man," Claude said. "And one more word of advice … well … let's make it two …

"First off, you keep your ass out of the Buccaneer, you hear?"

Chris nodded.

"And second, when you get your driver's license … don't you go endin' up like my man Jose did!"

Chris hugged him again, wondering if he would ever work with anybody quite like this fellow again.

Then, pulling a cigarette from the pack rolled in his shirt sleeve and strutting out like a heavyweight champion heading toward the ring to dispatch another bum, Claude disappeared out the doorway and down the stairs. After all, the weekend was here!

And so, Chris was left with the tester. There wasn't much for them to say. Chris felt like crying, but there was no way he could let himself do that in front of the man who gave so much of himself to him.

"You take care of yourself, kid," he said. "I don't want to see you back here."

Chris couldn't help it. He hugged the tester, and this time, he was the strong one.

"Damn," the tester said, looking in his shirt pocket. "Now you owe me two cigars."

Those were the last words Chris heard him say. They laughed, and the tester punched Chris in the arm, mussed his hair, tapped him on the shoulder and walked away, headed back upstairs.

Chris was never sure, but he thought he saw the tester rubbing his eyes on the way, just before Chris, who was doing the same, turned and ran down the stairs, his back to the Blake for the last time.

BOOK
THREE

28: A VISIT TO THE RUINS

There are places where things rarely every change, and the streets in Chris Tiller's old hometown hadn't changed much in the three decades since he had walked them as a teenager.

Oh sure, most of the sidewalks were broken and cracked now, and nobody seemed to be in a hurry to fix them. The roads themselves were even bumpier and had more potholes than they had on those mornings and evenings when his Dad had driven him to and from work.

The little corner grocery stores were mostly gone, either boarded up, or torn down. Most of the corner taverns were closed up, and the ones that were still in business had a tired look about them.

The endless row of used car dealers he used to pass by were fewer in number now, and the ones that were there seemed relatively lifeless compared to what they were like in the old days.

Houses still lined the streets, but most seemed to be badly in need of repair. Rare was the roof that didn't need patching, and on many of the houses, the aluminum siding was dirty and dented from years of rain, hail, and snow.

Once in a while, there was a new fence, but mostly they were either rusted old chain-link models, or wooden fences missing at least a few pickets.

Rusted-out or broken-down playground sets, or dismantled old bicycles reminded passersby that children once played in the yards behind these houses.

Chris steered his new Oldsmobile through these streets one summer Saturday morning in 2001, with his sons Derek, who was ten years old, and Tyler, who was eight, in the front and rear seats, respectively.

The boys had not grown up in this town, and had volunteered to go with their father for a ride rather than wait for their Aunt Louise to finish cooking what would be an early dinner at her house before they headed home, which was now about two hours away.

Chris rarely visited his old hometown anymore, but he and his sister had some family business to go over, and he had been curious as to what some of his old haunts were like after all these years.

For the most part, the boys were oblivious to his tour-guide-like description of what the town used to be like. The town meant nothing to them. But as the Oldsmobile started to ascend a hilly street, they took notice as he talked about his previous trips up that path.

"So, how would you guys like to have to walk up this hill every day just so you could go to work for eight hours … and in a factory, too!"

"You did that, Dad?" asked Derek. "How come?"

"How come I had the job, or how come I walked?"

"Both!"

"Well, back in those days, all my friends were working and making money, and I never had any, so as soon as I could, I wanted to get a job. The job I had up here was the only one I could get … or the first one, anyway."

"How far was it from grandma's house?"

"About a half an hour," Chris said. "If I was working at night, I had to walk to work, up this hill. If I was working during the day, I got to go downhill."

"No walking uphill both ways, then?" joked Derek.

"No, smart guy! And your grandfather did give me a ride either to or from work, so I didn't have to walk at night. Even back then, that could be a little dangerous."

The Oldsmobile rocked a bit as it completed its climb up the pot-holed street. Chris smiled slightly at the thought of the bumpy ride.

"Don't jostle 'em," the voice said in his head.

As they reached the top of the hill, he saw the outline of what was left of the old mill. He hadn't been sure if it was even still there, since the building certainly could have been torn down by now. But it hadn't been, and there it sat, off to the right at the top of the hill.

He pulled into the parking lot, now riddled with cracks and divots in its asphalt. Weeds poked out from those cracks and divots, and at the back edge of the parking lot, the weeds had grown so tall that the wooded area behind it was hardly visible.

There were maybe six or seven cars in the lot. It was the least-occupied Chris had ever seen it. Back during his summer at the Blake, the lot was almost always filled, even at six in the morning, with the guys from the graveyard shift parked there, and the early birds, fellows such as Will, already there for the start of the day shift.

"Dad, why are we parking here?" Tyler asked from the rear.

"Did you used to live around here or something?" Derek added.

Chris turned off the engine and looked around. He couldn't focus on anything in particular; his mind was being tugged at from every direction, it seemed.

"You guys wait here, and don't get out of the car unless I tell you to," he said. "I'll leave the windows open, and I'll only be across the street there if you need me."

The prospect of sitting in a stuffy Oldsmobile, parked in a grungy parking lot outside of some old building on the top of a bumpy hill in a grimy town that they were told had some special significance to their family, well, it didn't exactly excite the two boys. But they could tell their father was on some sort of mission, the importance of which apparently only he could comprehend.

So as the two boys started to sweat in the Oldsmobile, Chris Tiller, a fortysomething television and radio executive who for the past twenty or so years had worked in an air-conditioned office and eaten his lunch at really nice restaurants, began to search for the ghosts of a time when he worked in this sweaty block of a building and ate his brown-bag lunch while sitting on a rock.

He made his way to the front door.

29: NOBODY ELSE TO ASK

The first thing he saw was a dirty square off to the side of the door. He immediately recognized it as the spot where the brass sign had been.

The sign once had said "Blake Silk Mill," and when Chris first saw it, the latter two words had been labeled over so that it read "Blake Textiles."

But the brass sign was long gone. Only the dirt that had accumulated under it for decades remained, painting a permanent stain on the old building. Now, just an ugly, small square of clear acrylic sat in its place, and on it had been painted a cryptic message.

"Z3 Industrial Storage"

Chris had no idea what that meant, but it obviously was the name of the new tenant of the old mill.

Looking toward the roof, he searched in vain for the big block letters that once advertised the presence of the mill for miles around. There was nothing up there now to scream from the rooftop, and the letters, no doubt, had long since been melted down or otherwise recycled.

He left the entrance area and began to walk around the aging building. There was no sign of any activity anywhere.

A few old boxes were stacked on the loading dock, but there was no sign of any urgency to move them in or out. In fact, all but one of the loading dock doors had been bricked over.

Where once an entire team of shippers worked day and night unloading the raw materials for the mill, and loading the results of its efforts, out of and into huge trailers and boxcars, there was almost nothing.

He couldn't remember ever seeing the loading dock empty. Back in his day, there was always at least one boxcar on the railroad track parallel to the dock. But now the track was covered by weeds. And it didn't matter anyway, because about twenty feet from the dock, a chain-link fence had been erected; no trains had traveled on these tracks for years.

He noticed some of the old transformers and generators that had helped power the mill; the transformers looked to be in disrepair, and he feared what toxic substances might be leaking from them.

The generators were rusted, and obviously hadn't been fired up in years.

Wandering around, he saw few signs that anything was actually taking place inside. Was it a warehouse? A glorified corporate storage facility? Or did somebody just buy it as a tax write-off, letting it sit empty in perpetuity?

He went back up toward the front door and tried to open it, but it was locked.

"What's he trying to do, break the door down?" Derek asked his brother from the Oldsmobile.

After a few tugs, Chris gave up on the door. He wondered if the heavy glass window was still there, the one behind which so many conversations pivotal to the lives of the people at the mill had taken place. What had become of those big, heavy wooden desks they all used. The manual typewriters? The old, heavy telephones? The glass-tanked water cooler?

He sighed, knowing he would get no answers to those questions in this place. The ghosts of the Blake Silk Mill, if in fact there were any, were not giving anything up, he thought.

So he turned his back to the door and, reaching into his pocket for his car keys, took a few steps back toward the car.

"Thank you!" said Derek as he saw his father approaching.

But then, something made Chris look over to a corner of the building. And there, in a dingy, yellowing white suit of overalls, was a little man, probably in his seventies, carrying a small trash can to what looked to be the only remaining dumpster on the premises.

Chris rubbed his eyes, wondering if he actually had seen life. The man dropped the contents of the trash can into the dumpster, and then, surprisingly, with a wave of his hand, motioned to Chris to join him.

He wasn't sure who the man was. But he kind of wanted to find out what was going on at the place these days; who owned it, what they did now, and so on.

And there wasn't anybody else around to ask.

30: BROTHER, CAN YOU SPARE THE TIME?

"Hey there, if you're looking to sell somebody something, you ain't gonna find anybody there today," the old man said. "They only got one or two part-time people, and they sure ain't gonna be there on a Saturday."

Chris looked at the man as he approached him. He assumed the man was some sort of janitor or custodian, but he could also have been some sort of watchman, and he had no intention of getting arrested for trespassing at his old textile mill.

"No, I was just curious about what they were doing here nowadays," he said. "I used to work here when I was a kid, and I haven't been back up here in about thirty years. I was wondering what became of the place, or if it was even still standing."

"Well, you can see it's still standing," said the old man, putting down his trash can, and wiping the sweat from his brow after removing his tattered cap. "But it ain't been a silk mill for … oh, I guess about ten, maybe fifteen years now."

"Went out of business, huh?"

"Yes and no," said the old man, pulling a cigarette out and lighting it with a World War II-era lighter. "Didn't exactly go out of business, from what I hear. Just moved the whole operation somewhere in South America, Colombia, or Venezuela, or one of them places."

"And the people who worked here?"

"Don't work here no more, obviously," the old man said. "Ain't sure what happened to most of `em."

Chris looked at the man's face, and for a moment, he thought he saw something familiar. The man's nose, his chin, his whole facial structure; had he seen this fellow somewhere before?

But what he couldn't place were the man's eyes. For a craggy, old custodian or watchman, the man had eyes that were … well, they were warm, friendly, almost inviting. He seemed to be the kind of guy who could be friends with anybody.

"So, you worked here back in the old days, eh?" the man said. "Did you work in the mill, or out back, or what?"

"I was a bobbin boy," Chris said.

"Oh, a bobbin boy, eh? Never quite figured out what you fellows did in there, but I guess it was important."

Chris smiled, and reached out his hand to the old man.

"Chris Tiller," he said. "Nice to meet you."

The man took his hand, shook it warmly, and with that familiar face and those inviting eyes, calmly introduced himself.

"Nice to meet you," he said. "My name's Jimmy O'Hara."

31: REQUIEM FOR A WAY OF LIFE

Chris looked at the man, then chuckled somewhat nervously.

"Jimmy … Jimmy O'Hara. That's … that's really funny."

"What's funny about it … typical Irish name!"

"Well, I know, but it's funny … you being the only one here and all … I mean … Back when I worked here, we had a … one of the bosses here was …"

Jimmy smiled, as if he knew what Chris was driving at.

"A little floorlady, that's who you talkin' about?"

Chris felt something pop in his brain; if he didn't know better, he would have thought he was having a stroke. He recovered in a few seconds, but he still was trying to process what he just heard.

Then he looked at Jimmy again. Yes sir, it was all there. The same nose, chin, and features. Everything but the eyes. These eyes, they were *so* different. Could it be?

"You're talkin' about my big sister, I guess," Jimmy said. "Well, lookin' at it the way we look at it, anyways, you're talkin' about somebody who *used to be* my big sister."

Chris felt something, some emotion, wash over him. He was noticeably shaken.

Jimmy motioned Chris over to a small bench nearby. He sat down, lit another cigarette with the ancient lighter, and motioned for Chris to sit next to him.

Putting his hand on the younger man's knee, Jimmy began to speak, and suddenly, there was no 1971, nor was there a 2001. Everything was suddenly one large flow of time and space and people, and the perceptions of three decades began to wash away as Jimmy spoke.

"First off, like I said, Blake pulled out of this place back a few years ago. It wasn't that much of a surprise, I guess. Lots of other factories around here closed before that. You could drive around this town all day and you'd need an adding machine to count them up. Whatever we used to make in this town ... sewing machines, truck motors, record albums, tablecloths, whatever ... they all got sent off to Mexico or someplace like that. Wasn't any way to stop it.

"They shut this place down and it just sat here, waiting to rot like the Rogers plant ... you seen that lately?"

Chris shook his head. The massive Rogers mill had been the real giant of the local textile industry.

"Well, it's deserted now. All the lettering and all the statues and everything up on the building, all gone. All the windows busted up. They had a couple of fires in there from all the bums sleeping in there overnight. Lots of drugs and stuff in there, too, from what I hear. They'd be better off just blowing the place up."

Chris had a classmate who had worked at Rogers a year or so after he'd worked at Blake; in its prime, Rogers ran shifts around the clock, its machinery maintained on the fly.

Now, according to Jimmy, it was an eyesore.

"They got lucky here," Jimmy continued. "Well, the owners, anyways. They got this bunch to come in and use what was left as a warehouse. It took `em months to get all those machines out of here; not sure what they did with most of `em, but they're gone."

"So it's empty in there now, where all the machinery was?" Chris asked.

"Oh yeah, except for about half of the third floor. That's where they store whatever they store in there. Tell you the truth, I ain't even sure what they got in there."

"So who works in there now?"

"Oh, about a dozen … well, maybe more like twenty … folks, mostly men, but a few ladies, too. About once a day, in the evening, a truck comes in, and drops off a load, and then picks up a load. That's it, actually. Down to one truck a day."

"Doesn't sound like much of an operation."

"It ain't. They got me to keep the lights on and the furnace going in the winter, that and takin' out the trash. Couple of part-time gals in the office. That's about it."

Chris looked at the building. There had been so many facets to the operation before; his area was just a small part. Now, it was like an old steam engine left to rust in a railroad museum.

"Any idea what's up on the top floor?" he asked.

"Oh, no, that's sealed off," Jimmy said. "I ain't never been up there. I guess they had all sorts of chemicals and stuff up there."

"Yeah, they sure did."

"You been up there?"

"Oh yeah, lots of times, back in the old days. I was … well, the fellow who worked up there, I was kind of his assistant one summer. I'm sure he had a lot of kids doing that at one time or another, but I sure liked working with him. He kept that bitch … ooh, sorry, I forgot …"

"It's okay, you was gonna say 'that bitch Maggie O'Hara,' weren't you?"

"Yeah, but I forgot …"

"Well, I guess this is as good a time as any to tell you about her. Ain't nothin' else for me to do here today, really. But you better get prepared to hear something you didn't expect, okay?"

Chris shook his head, while Jimmy lit another cigarette. He took a long drag – it kind of reminded Chris of another long-lost acquaintance from the Blake, Richie – and started talking, staring straight ahead, and not at Chris seated next to him.

"Now, then, you said you worked here what, about thirty years ago?"

"Yeah, in 1971."

"Well, about that time … you ever go down past what they used to call 'Used Car Row,' down the road here?"

"Did I? I used to walk past there every day I worked here. If I was on the night shift, I walked past it on my way here. If I was working days, I'd go by on my way home."

"Well, then, son, you walked right past me. Back then, I was one of the top salesmen at old Geneva Motors. You remember them?"

"Sure. My old man bought a car or two there over the years."

"He always drove used, eh?"

Chris nodded.

"Just like lots of folks around here … strictly used! Anyway, I worked there a long time. Made good money there, in fact. Yes sir, I'm sure there must have been a time when you walked by there and you saw me there, hair slicked back, smart tie on," Jimmy said, adjusting an imaginary tie as he spoke.

"I'm sure I was setting somebody up in one of those … well, sometimes we called them 'shit boxes,' but they weren't all bad, those used cars. It was kind of like rollin' the dice, you know. Sometimes you got a lemon, and sometimes you got a pretty decent car out of it.

"But yeah, that was me. Got that job right out of high school. My folks were glad to see me get it, too. Glad that I didn't, the way they used to say it, 'take after that damned Maggie.'"

Jimmy could tell Chris was shocked to hear that.

"Got you on that one, didn't I? Okay, well, no sense dragging this out any longer. But first, why don't you tell me a little bit about my big sister, the one you wanna call 'bitch'?"

"I … I really shouldn't," Chris said.

"No, go on," Jimmy said. "It'll make more sense when you hear what I have to say."

Chris took a deep breath and thought back three decades. Even after all that time, the anger still simmered.

"I hate to say it like this, but she *was* a bitch," he said. "It wasn't so much that she was hard on us; that was her job, I guess. It was just that she never let up, never stopped telling us what we were doing wrong. For Christ's sake, she got in my face on my last ten minutes I was here!"

"That ain't surprising," said Jimmy.

"She had the nastiest eyes I've ever seen," Chris continued. "Evil, almost. Even if she wasn't yelling or saying something mean to you, the look in her eyes … it was like some sort of wild animal looking at you.

"And she never could mind her business. I would be talking to somebody and she would interrupt. I saw her make grown women cry, and I saw her treat … we had some retarded guys working here back then … and I saw her treat them like they were monkeys or something.

"There were only two fellows she didn't mess with. And they were the two fellows I remember the most … one was a black fellow named Claude. Any idea what happened to him?"

Jimmy pursed his lips and nodded his head.

"Not sure, but I know a fellow who worked here got shot dead one night at one of the bars downtown … about five, six years ago. But it could've been another one, I guess."

"Yeah, I guess," Chris said.

"The other guy was the one who worked up on the top floor. His name was Floyd. Ever hear of him?"

"Can't say as I have," Jimmy said.

"Well, your sister didn't mess with them," Chris said. "I think she was afraid of Claude because he was … well, he was a tough fellow and he did a lot of work.

"And Floyd … well, he knew the owners … you know, the Blake family … he knew they thought he couldn't be replaced, because he was the only one who knew the formula to treat the fabric, you know? And he was right.

"But anyway, that was Maggie. I have to tell you, I hated her then and I still hate her now … I don't like saying that … but it was just … just the way she treated people, it was …"

"Like a bitch?"

"Yeah. Like a bitch."

Jimmy nodded and smiled. He took a deep breath and looked up at the sky briefly.

"I can see that, given you only knew her from here," he said.

"You mean, she was different when she wasn't here?"

"Well, not once she got here. But there was a time …"

Jimmy got up and started to pace while Chris stayed seated.

"What if I told you that when I was a little guy, I had a sister who was an 'A' student, who was one of the best piano players in the whole state … she won contests and everything … and who everybody said would go on and be a Miss America?"

Chris shrugged.

"Well, I did. She could play … you ever hear that … what they call it, that 'Sonata,' the one by the German fellow?"

"Beethoven?"

"Yeah, him."

"Moonlight Sonata?"

"Yeah, that's it," Jimmy said, humming a few notes. "She played it better than anybody you'd ever hear, before or since. And she was everybody's little darling. People wondered if she was going to go to Hollywood and be in the movies. The rest of us, we were just Maggie's brothers or sisters. She was the star … no doubt."

"Are you talking about …"

"Our folks sent her to Windwood Academy. It's closed now, but back then, it was *the* private girls' school around here. And it cost a fortune. I don't know where they got the money, but I know the rest of us never had any new clothes, and we were always behind on the rent. Our father never got a car at all, at least until I got into the business and got him one out of my own pocket.

"But what money we had, I know, it went to pay the tuition at Windwood."

"Was that for …"

Jimmy kept talking, not really paying attention to whether Chris was listening.

"She was going to go to college, and she was the only one in the family they ever considered sending off. She more or less had her pick of some of the better ladies' colleges; they all wanted her, or so I was told. But then …"

Jimmy turns toward the building.

"Then she came here!"

Chris looked at the building as well. He was confused. Was Jimmy really talking about Maggie?

"She just wanted to make a little money for herself over the summer before she went back to her senior year at Windwood. The folks figured it couldn't hurt, so they went along with it.

"About three, four weeks into the summer, we all noticed a change. She stopped playing the piano, pretty much. She never talked about going back to school. She got an attitude about her, picked up bad habits, and things just got terrible at home."

"So what the heck happened?" said Chris.

"That son of a bitch she met in here," Jimmy said, pointing to the mill. "George Cunt-fer or whatever the hell his name was!"

It was as if Chris had been hit on the side of the head. *GEORGE!* He'd almost forgotten about *him*! But obviously, Jimmy and his family had not.

"George … I know he and Maggie were tight, but …"

"TIGHT!" roared Jimmy. "We never knew for sure, but the son of a bitch must have started fucking her right after she got here. Whatever the hell he did, he turned that girl around like you wouldn't believe."

"I … I can't imagine what George could have done …"

"Well I can!" said Jimmy. "He was the first fellow she met who wasn't … how could I say it? … who figured he wasn't below her standing. First one I guess who wasn't intimidated by her, at least by how smart and talented she was. I guess he was some sort of half-assed manager and for the first time in her life, I guess, she looked up to somebody … even if he was an asshole."

"And he sure was!"

Jimmy pounded one fist into another as he talked about George.

"One of the things that happened was, she started to take on that son of a bitch's personality. Believe me, man, she wasn't like that before. If she acted like a bitch to you and your co-workers, it was because she was around that son of a bitch so much!"

"Did anybody ever try to do anything about it?"

"Oh man, my old man threw that son of a bitch out of the house, told him never to come around again. But she kept running off to meet him. In fact, she started hanging around here when she wasn't working. She never did go back to finish school because he talked her into working here full time. And once she did that, she started picking up all his bad habits.

"If she saw him act like an asshole to an employee, she did it too. And if he screwed something up, and found somebody else to blame it on, she would back him up. I heard lots of stories, believe me."

Chris thought back to the tester's musings, as to what the relationship between George and Maggie really was.

"So anyways, she never went to college, of course. All that money on piano lessons and private school, down the drain. My folks kicked her out and she went to live in one of those ladies' rooming houses, and she lived there a long time … probably was still there when you were here."

"Why didn't she …"

"Move in with him? Because first off, he was a mama's boy, a bully in here, but a pussy around his mama. He couldn't bear to leave her alone, and she … his mama, I mean … would throw a fit if he even talked about it.

"Plus, his mama … she wouldn't have Maggie around because of …"

Chris bristled at what he thought was coming next. Jimmy started to shake.

"Yeah, she got knocked up, all right. And that … son of a bitch … he made her …"

This time, Chris knew what was coming next. He put his hand on Jimmy's to steady it.

"… he made her get a God-damned abortion!" Jimmy said.

They both went quiet for a moment.

"Did she … did she ever try to get him to marry her?"

"Shit no!" Jimmy roared. "But then again, thanks to whatever sick shit he put in her head, Maggie decided that if she wasn't going to marry George, she wasn't going to marry anybody. So, in a sense, she got married to this fucking place, where at least she could be around him. It was a fucking disaster!"

Chris thought for a moment. He tried to visualize the Maggie that Jimmy was describing, the sweet, intelligent, talented child prodigy who might have gone on to a happy life, had she not wandered into the Blake one day and hooked up with George.

He wished, if only for a moment, that he could have known *that* Maggie. He should have known there was some dark secret behind those dark eyes.

"So Maggie, she worked here 'til they shut this place down … well, at least the mill part," Jimmy said, calming down. "She was lost after that for a few weeks. Then, well, then she found out she had that Alzheimer's … you ever heard of that?"

Chris nodded.

"Makes you more or less lose your mind, you know? Maybe it's God's way of righting the things we do wrong in life … I don't know. The funny thing is, because of that, Maggie don't remember anything about this place. She don't know who George is, she don't know what the Blake was, and she wouldn't know a bobbin boy from Santa Claus. She don't remember anything about no baby. In some ways, it's like she is that innocent little girl again.

"The other day, I went over to see her ... I'm the only family she has left, you know? They gave her an ice cream cone. You ever see when a little kid, say four or five years old, gets an ice cream cone, how happy they get? Like it's all that matters in the world? That's how Maggie is now. She's back to where she was before the piano lessons, before the private school, and before ... before George! In some fucked-up world of her own."

This was not what Chris expected to hear on his visit back to the Blake. The boys, not knowing what was keeping him, had already violated his edict not to get out of the car, and were running loose in the parking lot. But Chris hardly noticed.

"There was another guy Maggie worked with, some Italian fellow," Jimmy said.

"Tony?"

"Yeah, I guess so. They say he's got that Alzheimer's too. Shit, man, let's hope there ain't something in the air here."

Chris hoped not, at least for Jimmy's sake.

"So what about George?" he asked. "Any idea what happened to him?"

"Oh, he's long gone," Jimmy said, almost cheerfully. "Son of a bitch didn't make it past six months after this place closed. Dropped dead one day in his backyard ... actually, the backyard he inherited from his mother. I don't know who went to the bastard's funeral. Maybe Maggie did. No way to find out now, I guess.

"I hate to speak ill of the dead, but I guess I already have been," Jimmy said, shrugging. "Anyway, with that piece of shit, good riddance, as far as I'm concerned."

Chris looked around, and a sense of mortality started to grip him. Maybe it hadn't been such a good idea to come back to the Blake, or what had been the Blake. He had assumed that a lot of the people he worked for or with there might be dead or not doing well, but to hear it made official, from this custodian-turned-historian named Jimmy, well, it was a bit unsettling.

Somewhere out there, he knew, somebody knew the story of what really had happened to Claude, and to poor little Richie. Was Shirley now an old woman somewhere, but still something of a hottie despite her years? Was Will sitting in a rocking chair somewhere, still gabbing away in his gold chains and white shoes?

Was little Jeff still a hippie? Had Andy and Carol continued their relationship past the affair stage? Did Brian actually ever become a minister?

And of course, he wondered about the tester, Floyd. He really wished he could find out what happened to him. He was the first one to predict this would happen, how the old silk mills would turn to rust.

Chris wondered how many other young men had wandered into the Blake over the years, and had the tester take them under his wing? Had any of the others quit to start football practice, only to end up being cut from the squad within a week? Did any of them take up the offer to work at the mill at night? Where would he, Chris, stand on the totem pole of the tester's protégés?

One thing for sure, he thought. Wherever Floyd was now, there were parts of him all over this town, somewhere, and maybe all over the country and part of the world.

Nobody who encountered him, from his mentor, the chemist, to the last bobbin boy he saved from Maggie, would ever forget him.

"I see you're kind of taking a walk down memory lane here," Jimmy said. "I hope I didn't startle you too much, but I figured you'd want to know."

"I did," Chris said. "Thanks for telling me."

They both stood up and shook hands. And Chris looked him in the eyes one more time. It was the closest he could ever get to looking into the eyes of the Maggie that had been, the pre-Blake, pre-George Maggie. A girl he wished that maybe he could have known.

"You take care," Jimmy said.

"You, too," said Chris. "If it's at all possible, tell your sister I said hello, and that I'm sorry."

Jimmy nodded and walked away as Chris headed back toward the parking lot.

"I thought I told you guys to stay in the car!" he shouted to the boys.

"Well, you were too busy talking to that old guy," Derek said. "It could be considered child abuse to leave us in there that long, you know!"

With a wave, Chris herded the boys back into the car and started the engine, all set to drive away for good.

But of course, there was one other memory to explore. Somewhere, beyond that thirty-year growth of weeds, there had been a little clearing in the woods, and a small rock on which a sixteen-year-old boy not only sat alone day after day thinking about life, about his future, and about the world, but it was also where he was transformed, even if only a tiny bit, into what would become a successful father, and man.

He looked back to where he thought the rock had been. His throat got dry, as it always did when he was anywhere near her.

He never knew her name, or anything about her back then. He sure wasn't going to find out anything about her now.

But as he got in the Oldsmobile and started to pull out of the parking lot for what he knew would be the last time, he looked at the Blake, and he looked at the wooded area, and he did something that he had done without fail, for every day of his life after that lunch break on his last day of work at his first summer job, something he knew he would keep doing, for every day of his life, until the day he died.

He thought about her.